Jake's heart thumped.

He realized he didn't want her to go. He'd become used to her being there. He even enjoyed their arguments. Sometimes he looked forward to them. But she had to be thinking of returning to work. And why wouldn't she? He'd taken her suggestions and he was better for them.

"Lauren, if you can postpone going until Cal returns, I'd like that."

Jake wanted to see Lauren, but he was driving and could only glance at her. She appeared at a loss for words. He didn't know if she expected him to say what he had. He hadn't intended to, but he liked talking to her. He liked her more than as a friend, but he couldn't let it go further than that. He remembered her first day, when she walked into the apartment and had to pry him out of bed. Now here he was asking her not to leave.

Dear Reader,

I've always loved masquerade parties, and writing *Healing the Doctor's Heart* gave me the opportunity to revisit that game. Lauren had to find a way of cracking the glass Jake had around his heart and her method proved unconventional to say the least.

New York City is also one of my favorite places to visit and I'm blessed to live so close to it. Setting the story there among the varied cultures and street figures that garner tourists' attention was perfect. But the characters of Lauren Peterson and Jake Masters warmed my heart. They are part of my growing family of people I want to talk to time and time again. I want to know what happens to them next. Do they have children? How does Lauren handle a new baby? The book could go on and on and on, but there are other stories to write.

I'm working on another one right now and hopefully you'll be ready to read the story of Jake's brother soon.

Thanks for going on the adventure with Jake and Lauren, and if you're interested in this and other books I've written, you can contact me through my web page or on social media.

Thanks again and as always, keep reading.

Shirley Hailstock

HEARTWARMING

Healing the Doctor's Heart

—

Shirley Hailstock

ISBN-13: 978-1-335-88955-3

Healing the Doctor's Heart

Copyright © 2020 by Shirley Hailstock

Shirley Hailstock began her writing life as a lover of reading. She likes nothing better than to find a quiet corner where she can get lost in a book, explore new worlds and visit places she never expected to see. As an author, she can not only visit those places, but she can be the heroine of her own stories. The author of forty novels and novellas, Shirley has received numerous awards, including a National Readers' Choice Award, a Romance Writers of America's Emma Merritt Award and an *RT Book Reviews* Career Achievement Award. Shirley's books have appeared on several bestseller lists, including the *Glamour*, *Essence* and *Library Journal* lists. She is a past president of Romance Writers of America.

Books by Shirley Hailstock

Harlequin Heartwarming

Summer on Kendall Farm
Promises to Keep

Visit the Author Profile page
at Harlequin.com for more titles.

CHAPTER ONE

DR. LAUREN PETERSON's feet pounded the New York City sidewalk with the same force as her heartbeat. The point of no return was still ahead. She should turn around, dash down the steps to the subway and go back to the Brooklyn brownstone she was giving up at the end of the month. She still had time. No one would know. No one would be hurt. Disappointed, maybe, but not hurt.

She could almost feel herself doing it, reversing course and heading home, the ghost of her skirt plastered to her legs in the wind as she made her attempt to run away from what she was hurtling toward. The traffic, pedestrians all seemed to crowd around her, slowing her footsteps.

"This is the stupidest thing I've ever done," Lauren said out loud. Since her decision was dumb and foolish, she had no problem having people on the street thinking the same about her.

Maybe she should care.

Why had she allowed Caleb Masters to go on interviewing her for that job, especially when she realized Jake Masters wasn't there? She stopped abruptly and looked at the sky. Two people careened into her and she backed up against a building, accepting their angry looks as she let them pass.

"What was I thinking?" This time her voice was barely above a whisper, since she knew the answer could come from only her own mind.

People around her moved aside, giving her plenty of room. Many looked curiously at her. She was talking to herself without a phone near her mouth or earbud cords streaming down to some concealed electronic device. Thankfully, she was clean, well dressed and carrying shopping bags, but that wasn't proof that she had all her faculties.

Resuming her steps, Lauren thought of the recent interview with Caleb, only two days ago. She'd gone to it hoping Jake would be there, as well. It was her way of reconnecting with him. They hadn't met in years. She was going to explain who she was, but that approach changed when the only person in the room was Caleb. She should have left before she made the mistake of asking about Jake, explaining that they went to college together. Caleb's interest piqued when she said that. Of course, she was Lauren Graves back then. Everyone called her Lori. Caleb then offered her the position. She accepted it and walked away.

And that was the stupid thing.

She objected to his argument that she was perfect for the job after she'd told him she wasn't a therapist. She was a pediatrician, dealing with children and overanxious mothers.

"He's seen too many doctors and refuses to see another one," Caleb said. That's when he told her he didn't want Jake to find out her profession.

She should have refused, left the room as fast as her spiked heels would carry her. Lauren didn't really want a job. Not now. She'd sold her practice. Her plans were to leave New York, move to a small town near the ocean or out west and reestablish her pediatric office. How could she let herself be talked into a job as a nonmedical aide for a man she hadn't seen in decades and conceal who she was? She was a doctor and proud of it.

And he was a broken man at that.

The schoolgirl crush she'd had on Jake Masters was preoccupying at the time, but she was an adult now, thankful that Jake was ignorant of her prior feelings. As a junior to her freshman in college, Jake didn't even know who she was. She was sure he wouldn't recognize her. But she wanted to see him anyway. She couldn't explain it other than to say she wanted to know if he was still as good-looking as he'd been in college and if that foolish crush she'd had on him was still there.

In the years since she finished school, she'd thought of him in passing, usually when she was online with a school chum, or if she went to a social event with college friends. In medical school, she wondered what he was doing. Once, she'd looked him up on the internet and found a reference that he was entered in a tennis tournament. He'd been good at athletics and she was surprised that he hadn't pursued that as a line of work.

Until Caleb told her Jake was a trauma surgeon, she wouldn't have thought the two of them had medicine as a common denominator. Now she was about to find out what else they had in common.

Lauren had reached that imaginary line.

HER HEART THUMPED the moment Jake came out of the office building. Caleb had said he was in. Looking down at the ground, seeing the imaginary line, she hesitated for a long moment, and then watched him moving toward her. Taking a deep breath, she rushed forward, the bags and packages in her hands swinging back and forth as she sped toward some pretend engagement. There were plenty of people on the street. Not only was it the end of the lunch hour, but also the tourists in this section of the city were thick and unpredictable.

Jake's head was down as he dodged the human traffic coming in all directions. Intentionally, Lauren bumped into him and like an actor on a stage, she bounced back, falling to the ground, her packages scattering everywhere.

"I'm so sorry," he said, offering his left hand to help her up.

Lauren pulled her belongings close to her as other pedestrians pushed her things back in the bags and handed them to her. Finally, she took Jake's hand and he levered her up. His hand was soft, but strong, a doctor's hand. She was surprised at the strength of him. Even though she knew that the loss of use in his right arm had likely strengthened other part of his body, she hadn't expected to feel so weightless as he pulled her into a standing position.

"Are you all right?" he asked.

She forced herself to breathe hard as she used her free hand to brush any street dirt from her skirt.

"I guess I'll live. I'm mostly embarrassed. My pride is a little injured but holding. It looks like my shoe bore the brunt of the physical damage." She hopped on one foot showing him the severed heel of her sandal.

"Let me get you a taxi," he offered.

She wondered how he was going to do

that if he didn't let go of her and use his left hand to signal for a cab.

"I don't need a taxi. I'm fine and I live in Brooklyn."

"The cost will be mine," he said. "After all, I wasn't looking where I was going."

She smiled. "I was walking too fast. How about we settle it with a cup of coffee." She looked behind him. Several shops, including a coffee bar, an Italian restaurant and a Greek eatery beckoned. "I have a new pair of shoes in one of these bags." She glanced down, lifting the bags slightly away from her. "I can change inside."

He looked around, probably noticing the eating places for the first time. Lauren could tell he wasn't exactly planning to spend any more time with her.

"I don't usually eat out," he said.

"I don't either, but I'm leaving the city soon and I'm trying out some new things before I head into the great unknown." She gave the last words an uptake of tone. "Come on, have some coffee with me."

"Well…"

She didn't give him time to refuse. Grabbing his left arm, she propelled him forward. "I'll even spring for the coffee."

He allowed her to pull him along, but when she neared the coffee bar, he stopped.

"This one would be more comfortable," he said. It was the Italian restaurant.

"You like Italian food." Lauren stated the obvious.

They went in. Lauren did her one-legged hop step as they followed the waiter to a secluded booth. The place was beautifully appointed. She felt as if she'd stepped from a New York street straight into Provence or Naples. Most of the tables were empty. Waiters had already begun preparing them for the dinner crowd. White tablecloths with bud vases holding a single rose, bone china and silverware gleaming in the light.

Luck was still with her as she settled her bags and placed her napkin in her lap. The line was crossed, and there was no going back, yet there were more hurdles for her to jump before she did what she'd been hired to do.

"Have you had lunch?" he asked.

She shook her head.

"They have some very fine food here. It's all made with fresh ingredients," he said.

So, he did know about the restaurants in the area. She'd been wrong in that. It was a mistake on her part. She'd have to be more alert in the future or he'd trip her up.

"I suppose that's how you like your food?" she said, just to have something to say.

He looked her straight in the eye for a long time. Lauren felt as if he was able to see into her mind. Then she realized the string of nurses and therapists he'd had in the past must have asked a question like that.

"You don't have to cut me with your eyes. I like fresh food too," she said.

He relaxed a bit. The waiter arrived and they quickly ordered.

"What's wrong with your arm?" she asked when they were alone again.

"You are certainly direct for someone I only met a moment ago."

She nodded. "You're right, especially since we haven't even exchanged names."

His expression told her he had yet to think of that small detail.

"Lauren Peterson." She extended her hand, her left hand.

Jake looked at it and after a moment pulled his hand up and shook hers. "Jake Masters."

"Now that we're acquainted, Jake Masters, what's wrong with your arm?"

"I had an accident."

"When?"

"I'm not going to play twenty questions with you."

"Too pushy?" she commented. He'd be amazed if he knew the shy, quiet college kid she used to be still lurked inside her. She was great with children, but it took a lot of courage for her to deal with adults who weren't the parents of her patients. And romantic relationships were out of her league ever since her divorce. "I'm sorry. I'm used to asking questions."

"Really, what do you do?"

His speech was very formal and he sat up straight in his seat, coming only short of folding his hands in front of him like he was in the third grade. Jake wasn't as warm and welcoming as his brother, and it made Lauren feel as if she was in another job interview.

"At the moment, I'm between careers."

"What did you do in your last career?"

She stared at him. "Arm surgery," she said.

A long moment went by and then he grunted. It wasn't a laugh, but a sound that told her he didn't believe her for a New York minute.

"And what are you going to do in your new career?"

"Now who's asking a lot of questions?" She paused. "Anyway, I haven't decided where to go yet. I'm looking at someplace close to the ocean. I've always liked the sea. I feel calm there. In the meantime, maybe I could work for you. Of course, it would be temporary."

"And why do you think I need someone to work for me?"

The waiter interrupted them with their meals. When he left, Lauren returned to the conversation.

"Because you're in pain and I know something about pain."

"How do you know I'm in pain?"

"By the way you're holding your shoulder." At that he shifted, but didn't truly relax.

"And by the way you clench your teeth until it eases."

She picked up her fork and took a bite of the seafood fettuccine she'd ordered. Closing her eyes at how wonderful it tasted, Lauren savored the pasta and sauce. She didn't often cook her meals with all fresh ingredients. She didn't have time. She remembered visiting her sisters and her parents. They always had *catch-up and cook time* in the kitchen. The five of them would catch up on what was happening in their lives while they made a meal. Their mom would plan the menu and each sister would choose what she wanted to make. It was a female bonding time that was fun and delicious. Lauren missed those days.

"Are you a therapist?" He nearly spit the word. The expression on his face was crafty.

"A massage therapist? Not technically, no. But I've done my share of working with someone in pain." She wiggled her fingers and smiled to show she knew what she was talking about.

"Don't bother. I'm fine. I don't need any kind of therapist," he said, again with a disdainful tone.

"I can see you're in pain, but…" Lauren raised and dropped her shoulders, leaving her statement open.

Jake said nothing. His silence made her only want to try harder.

"So, what do you do, Jake?"

He didn't immediately answer. "I'm between careers at the moment."

"I see," she said, knowing even with his dry method of speaking, he was mocking her. "I suppose in your last career you were a bouncer."

"What?"

"Someone who knocks people down on the street." Lauren wondered if he ever smiled. So far he'd scowled, winced and grimaced, but showed no positive emotion at all. He looked angry, something his brother had failed to tell her. Lauren had kept an image of him as the happy college student. But they were no longer in college and she was no longer Lori Graves. She was thirty-one and he was either thirty-three or thirty-four.

"That isn't it," he said.

She decided not to pursue it any further. Lauren was new to this pretend game and she didn't want to show her hand or let him discover that she'd been hired by his brother. She was naturally shy and nervous at all the talking she was having to do.

They ate in silence for a while, enjoying the excellent food. When the waiter brought the check, Lauren quickly took it. Without glancing at it, she handed him her credit card and he walked away.

"Not only pushy, but aggressive," Jake said.

"I said I'd pay for the coffee. The food came with it." She smiled again, hoping he'd reciprocate. She was disappointed.

The other diners finished and left the restaurant. Only she and Jake remained with the staff, who'd all but disappeared. Jake slid out of the booth. Lauren stood, still on one heel. When she saw that Jake was in pain, she placed her hand on his right arm. He stopped immediately, facing her.

"Let me help," she said in the same voice she always used with a crying child.

She didn't wait for his approval. In fact, she expected him to refuse. She began moving her hand along the length of his arm. With her thumb and forefinger, she worked long, steady strokes against his muscles, smoothly caressing them with both the heat and shape of her hands. It would be better if his arm was bare, but this would have to do, she thought.

Jake stiffened at her initial touch, but he relaxed as she added pressure from his shoulder to his wrist. Then using both hands, she pushed him into a seat. He didn't resist. Lauren found points where she assumed the pain was intense. Her fingers lingered there and she added releasing pressure to ease those tissues. His right arm was thinner than the left, indicating that he hadn't used it in a while and had not been exercising it according to any competent therapist's routine. She finished her impromptu massage, the entire procedure taking no more than five minutes. Stepping back, she stumbled, forgetting about her heelless shoe. With flailing hands she caught the table and steadied herself.

"Are you all right?" Jake asked whipping around, his good arm extended but couldn't have reached her in time.

"Fine." She smiled. "But I better put on those new shoes before I break an ankle."

Reseating herself, she pulled a shoe box from one of the bags and exchanged her broken heels for a pair of flat-sole shoes. When she stood, she was noticeably shorter than he was.

Outside, Lauren looked in the direction of the subway that would take her back to Brooklyn. She turned to Jake.

"Well, Jake Masters, thank you for the company. Consider the debt paid in full." She offered him her left hand. He took it and shook. Lauren wasn't sure, but she almost got a smile, at least the shadow of one at the edge of his mouth.

"It was interesting," he said, still in a formal tone.

Lauren felt like she should stand up straight and salute. She didn't know what his comment meant and decided not to find out if it was positive or negative.

"Well, Lauren Peterson, good luck with your new career."

Lauren opened her purse and pulled out a card. It had her name and a phone number on it. Handing it to Jake, she said, "Just in case you want someone to help alleviate the pain."

"Temporarily?"

She heard the sarcasm in his voice.

"True, so you'd better act fast or that number will be disconnected."

JAKE WAS SPEECHLESS. He hadn't been whirlwinded by a woman since…never? Had it ever happened? He couldn't remember. As he watched Lauren Peterson walking away, Jake wondered what had just happened. Who was she? She looked slightly familiar, but he was sure he didn't know her, didn't know anyone like her. Someone who could be both klutzy and aggressive at the same time. Women usually flocked to him. At least they had before… Jake stopped the thought. He wouldn't go there.

Since the accident, most people tried to ignore his arm. They didn't mention it, tiptoeing around even looking in that direction. If anyone approached him, they did it from the left. If he changed direction, they moved back to his left side, as if he had a contagious disease that would jump through the air and infect them.

Without even knowing his name, Lauren broached the subject of his injury head-on.

Jake admitted that threw him for a moment. He was in pain and when she bumped into him, it escalated.

There was no pain now. She said she wasn't a therapist, but her hands had felt magical as she soothed his muscles better than any licensed therapist had ever made him feel.

Who was she? he asked himself again. He had his eyes on her back. She walked confidently, weaving in and out of the swaying crowd. After a few seconds, she was gone, swallowed by the sea of humanity. Jake glanced at the card in his hand. It had her name and a phone number. He remembered her words. That line would be disconnected soon.

Pushing the card in his pocket, he told himself it didn't matter. He was no longer seeing therapists or nurses. They'd proved they could do nothing for him. It was all in his head. He'd been told that by the best psychologists in the business. Of course, they didn't use those words. They used medical school jargon to explain neurological deficits, paralysis or somatosensory losses. It was hysterical paralysis for the layman. He was no moron. He knew the language. He'd learned it alongside them in the same chairs at the same medical schools. In essence, his mind wouldn't let him move his arm.

Turning around, Jake dismissed Lauren. This was his life and this was how it was going to be. He headed toward the car that stopped at the curb. The driver got out and rushed around to open the door. Jake levered himself inside without any help and soon the car merged into the traffic.

Back at his apartment, the place felt cold and austere. It never had before. Had Lauren somehow changed his perspective? The apartment was a grand two-story space with twenty-foot ceilings and windows almost as tall, but today it felt empty and bleak. Lauren was different, not exactly a breath of fresh air, but someone he rarely came across. She was like spring: warm, sunny, colorful. Why was she making him feel that his apartment, the space he'd lived in for the last five years, was a grayed-out shell? It had everything he needed, furniture, lighting, paintings on the walls, books and a huge concert grand piano that had once belonged to his grandmother, yet he felt as if there was no life in the place.

Wasn't that the way he wanted it? As cold and empty as his life had become. Did the rooms reflect the state of his life? Had it atrophied along with his arm? Jake glanced at his right arm. The pain had not returned. He wondered what she'd done that was different from the multiple therapists who'd tried and failed. Why were her hands more effective than those of the professionals?

The pain was real, but phantom nevertheless. Jake stared at the limb that hadn't moved in two years. He willed it to move. Just a small change, even minuscule, would be welcome, his brain said. He'd ordered it to move millions of times since the doctors told him there was no physical reason why he shouldn't be able to use his arm. Yet it refused to answer the commands of his conscious brain. It hung limply by his side or stayed in a pocket if he used his left hand to put it there.

Since he'd stopped all the therapy, the arm was noticeably smaller than his left one. He could give himself all the rationalized reasons he wanted, but he knew that without ex-

ercising that arm, it would atrophy. He dug
out Lauren's card and looked at it. As he ran
his thumb over the raised lettering, he out-
lined her name, remembering her smile and
her touch. He could almost feel the warmth
of her hands sliding along the grain lines of
his muscles, coaxing them into submission,
giving them the blood flow they needed to
allow the natural biochemistry of the human
body to act as nature intended it.

His brother, Cal, came through the door
while Jake was still looking at the card.

"You're late," Cal said.

Jake knew his brother was concerned
about him. He wouldn't have been surprised
if Cal put out a missing person's report. In
this case, he probably only needed to contact the limousine driver to discover that he
was alive and well and talking to a stranger
on the street.

"I stopped for a late lunch with a woman
named Lauren Peterson."

"Really? Who?" Cal's brows went up in
surprise. Since the accident, Jake had spoken
to few women and agreed to no invitations.

Jake walked to his brother and handed
him the card. "Her. Check her out."

"Where did you meet her?"

"On the street. Actually, we ran into each other, literally. She fell, dropped her packages, then suggested we have a cup of coffee."

"Why am I checking her out?" Cal asked.

Cal always did the background checks. At least since the accident he had, taking on the role of protector to an infirm Jake. Jake was a wealthy man and he'd been taken advantage of once. Since then he protected himself. Jake didn't mind Cal looking out for him. He loved his brother and knew Cal loved him.

"You're concerned about me being alone while you go away. And since I refuse more nurses and therapists, at least for a while, maybe she will be the answer."

"Why do you think that? You've met her once. For the space of a lunch." Cal frowned.

"She massaged my arm and I'm not in any pain."

"What? Where? Did you two go somewhere?"

"Nope. Right there in the restaurant. We were about to leave and she started stroking my arm. The pain went away and so far it hasn't come back."

"And you let this happen?"

Cal knew how sensitive Jake had become to people touching him. Most of them didn't want to make contact. It was only the professionals who wanted to examine him, using the royal *we* to ask how *he* was doing.

"I didn't have much of a choice." Jake remembered how she'd begun. He would have stopped her, but the pain was subsiding and he couldn't refuse the relief.

"And you think this person you met on the street can fill the job."

"Not exactly I think she'll fill *your* requirement that there is someone here in case of emergency and to make sure I get to appointments on time. And that's why you get to do the digging."

"All right," Cal agreed. "I'll check her out."

"Cal." Jake's voice held a warning. "Don't veto her just because she isn't the nurse or therapy type you usually find."

"I'll be as thorough as possible. I don't want to be leaving you with a stranger who has no credentials."

"Don't make that sound like she might have a criminal record."

"I'll check that out too," Cal said as if the thought had just come to him.

Jake knew it hadn't, but he decided to ignore the comment. When his brother said he'd be thorough, he meant it. Both of them would need to know if she had a criminal record.

"One more thing, Cal. She said she's leaving the city soon, beginning a career somewhere else. That might be a problem."

"If all goes well, I'll contact her to see if she'll take the job, at least until I return." Caleb was a consulting engineer on a number of projects and traveled often.

Jake silently agreed with the plan. He just realized that he'd campaigned for Lauren. What was it about her that made him want to spend more time with her? They'd been in each other's presence for only two hours at the most and he was willing to spend time with her each day.

This was wrong, Jake thought. He didn't need anyone around to babysit him. He had a housekeeping staff that kept the place clean and a food service that managed his meals.

He had a driver to take him anywhere he needed to go. Even if Lauren checked out, he could let her go if he had to as soon as Cal left for his job.

And he couldn't be inconveniencing Lauren. She could go to her new place and begin her new career, whatever that was, sooner than she expected. It would work out for both of them.

However, before she left he'd get her to tell him what she did to his arm to relieve the pain.

CHAPTER TWO

LAUREN LOVED HER brownstone in Brooklyn.
It was three stories and a basement, long
with high-ceilinged rooms and character
that new homes couldn't come close to du-
plicating. But when she stepped through the
door of Jake's apartment, she felt that her
entire house could fit into a single corner.
She dropped her suitcase and a small thud
sounded, but no dust cloud rose up from the
magnificent carpet.

The housekeeper showed her to her suite,
a large bedroom with a king-size bed, a sitting room and her own bathroom. She'd been
there for an hour and she hadn't seen Jake yet.

She headed into the kitchen and found the
Mrs. Turner. The older woman had changed
her shoes and her purse hung from her arm.
She was obviously preparing to leave.

"Do you know where Mr. Masters is?"
she asked.

"Dr. Masters," she corrected. "I rarely see him. He spends a lot of time in his room. I come in three mornings a week and clean up, but I don't see him."

Lauren looked over her shoulder. From the kitchen she couldn't see the staircase that led to the second floor. Even if she could, she didn't know which room was Jake's.

"Well, good morning," the housekeeper said. "I have a key and I arrive around seven, but I can come later if that's inconvenient."

Lauren shook her head. "Seven is fine."

"I'll see you in a couple of days," she said.

With the closing of the door, Lauren was alone. The huge space felt like being inside an opera house, except the generous light coming through the windows made her think she was outside and not in a dark concert hall.

She wondered if Jake had a routine. Neither he nor his brother had mentioned anything except certain appointments that Caleb emphasized were important for Jake to attend. Lauren sighed. If he didn't have a routine, he was about to get one. Being alone too much was not good for him. She'd been pushy when they met. It was time for her to show him who was boss.

On her way up the stairs, she passed the rooms that had been assigned to her and went to the end of the building. If there was a master bedroom in the spacious apartment, it would probably be in one of the corners. She knocked on the door and waited. She heard nothing from inside. No movement, no radio's or television's muffled voices. Knocking again, she waited as the seconds ticked by.

On the third try, she knocked and opened the door simultaneously. She'd chosen the right door. The room was dark, curtains drawn and Jake lying in the massive bed. He didn't move as she came in, leaving the door open to let in light so she could see around any obstacles.

"Good morning, Jake," she said, using a stern voice.

He tugged the corners of his pillow over his ears. Again he didn't respond. This told her he was wide awake and ignoring her. She went to the windows and looked for a pull cord, but couldn't find one. Retracing her steps, she went around the bed, picked up a remote and pressed the power button. It would either open the curtains or turn on something electronic.

The drapes began to slowly open, letting in the eastern light.

"Close those." The gruff voice made her jump. Jake sat up in bed, throwing the covers back and turning toward her, all the while squinting at the light.

"Close those!" he shouted. Blinking, he looked at her. Lauren could tell he didn't recognize her at first.

"What are you doing here? I don't need some nanny showing up with her bag of tricks."

"You think I'm a person trusted enough to care for the well-being of children?" She thought about that for a moment. It gave her an idea. "Thank you."

"It wasn't a compliment."

"And just to be correct, I don't have a bag of tricks. What I do is pure magic."

"Really."

She smiled. "You never know." Taking a step toward the bed, she surveyed the room. "It is still morning. If you don't get moving, you'll barely make it downstairs before it's time for lunch."

"I don't want any lunch."

"I do, and I don't want to eat alone. So get up and get dressed. The housekeeper is gone for two days. This room smells like a gym and I imagine you do too."

Lauren didn't wait for a reply. She hurried out of the room, although she did leave the door open.

Twenty minutes later, he appeared in the kitchen. His hair was wet from the shower and he wore a wrinkled T-shirt, equally wrinkled shorts and no shoes.

"Let's get one thing straight," he began.

"That's a good idea," she interrupted him. "I'm here temporarily at the request of both you and your brother, so we need to have some ground rules."

"I—"

Her hand came up, palm out, stopping him. "The housekeeper says you rarely leave that room when she's here. From now on, you let her clean it." She gave him a piercing glance. "Toast and coffee are already made."

She poured Jake a cup and handed it to him. He took it and drank.

"I don't like black coffee," he said.

"Then you should have put your own cream and sugar in it." She indicated the items on the table.

"I also don't eat breakfast."

"I believe there is a list of things you don't do, but that will change."

"Oh?"

She raised one eyebrow. "You don't intimidate me," she told him. "Your brother filled me in on your accident and your attitude since then."

"I bet he did. Did he tell you I don't need or want a babysitter, not even a nanny who performs magic?"

"He also told me you don't want to see anyone, but you shouldn't be alone. And nanny or not, you've got me."

"Did he tell you that I might fire you the moment his plane left JFK?"

She nodded. Jake's eyes widened in surprise.

"He figured that would happen. So, he gave me a key and told me I should let you know that I work for him, not you."

"Meaning I have no fire power," he stated.

"That's the case." She smiled, feeling like

a fraud, but he didn't need to know that. "On the other hand, I have the right to leave at any time. And I'm sure you're planning to make my life miserable, so leaving will be my decision."

She got a grin out of him. It wasn't a full sardonic power play, but the shadow of what was apparent.

"So you'd better behave yourself. I can give as much as I get, Jake. Now, eat something. We're going out as soon as you finish."

Lauren took her coffee cup and scooted out of the kitchen. She made it up the stairs and into her room before her courage gave way. Letting out a long breath, she leaned against the closed door, and took long, calming breaths. She'd never spoken so candidly in her life. She wondered what was to come. Would Jake really make her life miserable?

He'd been different in the restaurant, but that was before she'd been sharing his life and his space. She would be staying in the apartment. The apartment was large enough for them to avoid each other, if he so chose, but as his companion she needed to interact with him. And he needed to interact with other people, as well. Her living here was convenient for her, too, as the couple she'd sold her brownstone to wanted possession as soon as possible.

Knowing that Jake was in pain and knowing that he really needed someone he could trust while Caleb was away. Lauren had to stay. He'd be abusive at first. She was sure of that. He was angry and she would get the backlash. Before coming here, she'd talked with a psychologist friend and told her what she planned to do without revealing the name of her... She hesitated. Could she call him a patient? She shook her head. She couldn't think of him as a patient. If she did, she might unintentionally refer to him that way.

Quickly, she unpacked her belongings and put them away. She didn't bring much. Everything she hadn't gotten rid of from the brownstone was in a storage unit, accessible, but not without inconvenience. Jake should have had enough time by now to get ready to go out. She hadn't decided where they were going when she issued the order. It was designed for one purpose—to let him know she wasn't going to be his doormat.

He was waiting in the living room when she came down the stairs.

"Where are we going?" he asked, his voice both gruff and challenging.

"For a walk in the park."

"Why?"

"You need the exercise."

"And you know this how?" he asked.

"When I bumped into you, you were so thin, I'm amazed you weren't the one on the ground."

"And you decided my welfare is now your responsibility?"

"I'm not here as one of your doctors." She had to remind herself as well as him. "But walking will give us time to talk, get to know each other, lessen some of the tension between us."

He eyed her keenly. She wondered if he was thinking again about how pushy she was. The thought made her feel powerful. She wasn't aggressive by nature, but she would allow herself to be pushed only so far before she pushed back. And Jake Masters was used to doing the pushing.

Not today, she told herself.

WHAT SHOULD HE FEEL? Jake asked himself. It had been so long since he'd felt anything but anger. And into his life plunges Lauren Peterson. If he wasn't so opposed to her intervention, he'd find the situation funny. Especially now that he was sitting and waiting for her, showered and dressed as she'd ordered.

It was ironic, he told himself. If Cal was here they'd both laugh at the absurdity of the situation. Jake had asked for Lauren. He had no idea she would be ordering him around.

He'd read the report Cal had left with him. She was an elementary school teacher. There was nothing else in the report that was of any interest. He didn't know exactly when she planned to leave the city, but since it was summer, school was not in session.

He heard the door open upstairs and looked up. The sun hit her and for a second his breath caught. Red highlights added a glow around her dark brown hair. He knew that color, knew another woman with hair the sun highlighted just like that. She'd been his first love—Pamela Bailey. He'd looked across his tenth grade classroom and saw the sun shining through Pamela's hair. Jake hadn't thought of her in years. What was happening to him? He was never usually this nostalgic.

Lauren was already on her way down the stairs and he followed her movements. She was taller than the average height for a woman, maybe five feet seven or eight. She wore pants that made her legs look as long as the Verrazano-Narrows Bridge. Her steps were measured and unhurried, making her appear regal. Definitely not the walk of any teacher he'd ever known.

"Are you in any pain?" she asked when she stood in front of him.

Jake hadn't thought of his pain since she accosted him in his bedroom. "I'm all right," he responded.

"Sit down and let me massage your arm before we leave."

"I thought you weren't here as a therapist."

"I'm not." She smiled. "But if you're in pain, you can let me help or you can suffer in silence."

He gave her a long look, but eventually sat down. She began to knead his arm, beginning at his shoulder. Jake allowed her touch to see if she could perform the same magic as the previous time. It was working. He could feel the warmth of her fingers.

"Are you sure you're not trained in this?"

"I'm self-trained," she told him.

"Self-trained? What does that mean?"

She waited a long moment. He felt her hesitate, then slightly ease the pressure of her hands. When she spoke, her voice was laced with suppressed emotion. "My mother suffered from severe migraine headaches and arthritis pain. I used to give her a massage every day."

"Every day?"

"It helped her."

She moved from his shoulder farther down his arm. Jake wore a short-sleeved shirt and her bare hands were on his bare arm. Heat penetrated his skin, seeping deep into his muscles and relaxing the tension. He wondered what she thought of his immobile limb. Had Cal told her anything about his medical history? What he'd been through? Would she understand?

"How does that feel?" she asked when she'd finished and stood back.

"Fine," he said. Jake held back how good

it felt. He refused to let her know that he wanted her to massage his arm any time he was in pain. He hated being dependent on people. He'd agreed to allow her to be his companion while Cal was away, just to get Cal off his back, but now he thought she could do more.

As long as she didn't interrupt his life. He'd have to have her agree to a few boundaries, *if* he could get a word in.

"Did the doctors find a treatment for her pain?" he asked.

"She died five years ago."

He turned to look at her. He could see why Cal had chosen her as his companion. She'd obviously gained good experience caring for her mother. Jake wanted to say something to ease her pain, but knew there was nothing that was appropriate or even wanted. All the platitudes that people came up with only made the person feel worse.

"I miss her. We had a wonderful relationship and I never minded giving her massages. It gave us time to talk and tell stories. I was her companion and caretaker."

Jake envied her the obvious love she had for her mother. He understood that love. His mother was the reason he'd gone into medicine. He'd followed in her footsteps and they were big shoes to fill.

"What does your mother do?" she asked.

"She worked as a nurse for years and now runs a nursing program at a university in Pennsylvania. My father teaches math at the same school."

"Do you see them often?"

"Not as often as they would like. Cal goes to see them more than I do."

"Why is that? You can't say it's your arm, since you can still walk and talk and I'm sure you can drive, even if you don't want to."

"Even before my arm, I traveled a lot or was seldom available except for holidays that might also be interrupted on a moment's notice."

"And now? It doesn't take both hands to pick up a phone."

"I call occasionally."

Jake was getting tired of her constantly mentioning his arm. He was so used to people doing their best to avoid the issue.

"Why don't we go for that walk you mentioned?" Maybe walking would give her something else to focus on.

And him too, because those auburn highlights kept sending his mind back to the days before the accident when he had his whole life before him. Now look at him. He glanced at his right arm. He used to go into operating rooms and save lives.

That was before he became useless.

THEY LEFT THE building through the arched doorway of the majestic Dakota apartment building on Central Park West. Jake wore a sling supporting his right arm. It was a short walk across the street to the park's entrance. Like most New Yorkers, Lauren crossed the street when there was a break in traffic, ignoring signal lights and taking her life into her own hands. Lauren stepped off the curb only to be pulled back by Jake.

A car rounded the corner and would have hit her.

"You're supposed to be *my* caretaker," he said. "Not the other way around."

"Companion. I am not a caretaker. That's a job I did not sign up for."

They crossed when the light turned green

and entered the park. The temperature was warm, yet pleasant, and for a while they walked without talking. Lauren was comfortable with the silence. The park was full of people. Children were playing on the vast lawn. There were tables where people sat playing board games and other places where a long curved bench ran the length of a fence. People sat there reading books or using their personal phones.

Lauren smiled as she and Jake passed by.

"It's been a long time since I walked in the park," she said.

Jake made a *hmm* noise that indicated he concurred. She wondered if he was warming up to her. The tension from the apartment seemed to have been left behind.

"Do you like parks?" she asked.

"Twenty questions again?"

"Just making conversation." She wanted to know more about him. "I take it you're a stick-to-the-subject type of guy." She huffed and used her arms to take a macho stance.

He laughed.

"That's the first time you've laughed since I met you."

He immediately dropped his head and his expression reverted to a stoic mask.

She couldn't resist. "Once it's broken, let the pieces fall away," she said.

"What?"

"You've smiled. The pieces that were holding your face in a scowl are gone." She imitated the cross way he looked. "You're much handsomer when you smile."

He stopped walking and stared at her. "Don't flirt with me."

"Flirt?" she said, honestly surprised. "I'm not flirting with you. If I were, I'd know it and so would you."

Tension returned between them.

After a few minutes walking in silence, Lauren slipped her arm through Jake's left one. He jerked at first. She knew he wasn't used to being touched. He probably thought people didn't want to touch him. She didn't let go, and pulled him along when he tried to stop.

"Not flirting," she said. When he didn't pull free of her, she decided to take another plunge. "Tell me about the accident."

"What?"

"Too soon?" she asked.

"Are you just nosy?"

She shook her head. "I think of it as getting to know you, knowing what happened and not having any subjects that are off-limits."

"Most people do this over time. You're trying to learn everything in one large information dump."

She laughed, still holding his arm. "Why wait? If there is a lot to know, getting it all at once could prevent me from stepping on your toes in the future."

"I have no idea what you mean," Jake said.

"I'm sure you do," she contradicted. "So why don't we start with the arm?"

She knew he didn't want to tell her about his accident. Maybe if she started with a lesser question, she could coax him into opening up.

"What did Cal tell you?" he said just as she was about to ask another question.

"That you were a surgeon and because of an accident a few years ago you can no longer move your right hand or arm." That hadn't been all Caleb had said, but Lauren wanted Jake to tell her his version.

"I was at a medical conference in France.

It was made up mainly of trauma surgeons. During a break, a few of us were heading for lunch at a local restaurant. Just before we got there..." He stopped talking and walking. Jake took a step away from her, their linked arms dropping in the process.

Lauren knew he was reliving the trauma. She could almost feel the lump in his throat. She wanted to give him some instructions on how to stop the memory, but she couldn't. She'd already told him why she knew how to massage as well as she did. That was the truth, but advising him on how to calm the memories of a trauma could tip him off that she knew more about medicine than a kindergarten teacher should.

After a moment, he resumed his story. "Terrorists happened next. A car plowed into a group of people on the street and detonated a bomb. I was one of the lucky ones. The concussion wave threw me against a building. The crush of bodies pinned me there until I couldn't breathe. When I woke, I was in a hospital. My shoulder and three ribs were broken. All have healed, except my arm." He looked down at the immobile limb.

"And you've been to a lot of doctors?"

"The best in the world," he said sardonically. "Cal saw to that, but no matter what they say, I still can't move my arm."

"It's not permanently injured?"

He looked her directly in the eyes. For a second his gaze showed vulnerability. He was afraid. The air around them seemed to change. It softened just as his eyes had.

"I don't know." His voice was barely louder than a whisper.

Lauren held his gaze although she wanted to look away. *I don't know.* He sounded like he could see into the future and that his arm would remain as it was today: in a sling against his shirt, without strength, mobility or usefulness.

The atmosphere turned maudlin and Lauren searched for a way to change it. She stepped closer to him and placed a hand on his arm.

"You resisted giving me a cliché when I told you about my mother," she said. "Allow me to return the favor."

His head dropped down a fraction.

"I won't say your arm will be better in the future, but…" She paused, knowing her next words could make the situation go either way. "It's not the end of your world, is it?"

"I'm a *surgeon*." His voice carried. Looking around, he checked to see if anyone noticed. No one paid any attention to them.

"I know you're a surgeon and you spent a lot of years in school honing your skills but there are other things you can do."

"Like what?"

"Teach," she said.

"This coming from a kindergarten teacher."

"Don't knock it. A lot of people taught you and I'm sure you credit at least one of them with helping you become a talented *surgeon*."

He said nothing, yet a perplexed expression crossed his face. Lauren went on. "You could write."

"With one hand."

"If necessary, but you could use a voice recognition program and hire an editor to make it readable."

"You don't think I can write?"

Lauren wondered if Jake was entertaining thoughts that he might do something else. His knowledge was still there. His dexterity might be impaired, but his mind was sharp. Of that she could attest.

"Most doctors can't. All they write are prescriptions."

"What would I write about?"

"Is that a trick question?" Lauren glared at him as if he was baiting her. Assuming that he wasn't, she answered. "You're a doctor. Write about medicine. Or write about your arm."

"A journal?"

"You could start with a journal and graduate to full books. Of course, a journal is personal. Writing one might help you."

"Do you keep a journal?"

"Not now," she said slowly.

"But in the past?" He left the sentence hanging.

"I did once." This time her voice was barely audible. "For a long time."

"Why?"

"Listen, I know from where I speak." She stopped him from delving into her life. She was his companion. He was not hers.

"I'll think about it," he finally said.

She heard no conviction in his voice. He was placating her. They walked on. Although his face gave nothing away, Lauren wanted him to focus on something other than his arm and the pain. She'd seen it happen in her pediatric patients. When she allowed them to play with the toys in her office and she asked them questions about what they were doing, they didn't focus on anything that hurt. Grown-ups weren't much different.

Jake was an enigma. She couldn't tell if he was bitter or just lost.

CHAPTER THREE

THE MOMENT LAUREN was alone, she called Amy Reynolds, her best friend and purveyor of all things. The two had known each other since Lauren opened her practice and hired Amy as her head nurse. Whenever a kid needed a hug or a toy, Amy seemed to find it within her arms or behind her back. It was uncanny how she could come up with the exact thing the child needed.

It also didn't hurt that Amy was in charge of office Christmas presents. All the staff loved her and her ability to find what was needed when it was needed.

"Lauren," she said when she answered her phone. "I've been thinking about you. How are things going?"

"They're a little tense at the moment."

"Not doing so good with the doctor?" she asked.

Amy was the only person who knew Lauren was working for renowned surgeon Dr. Jacob Masters. She'd been sworn to secrecy.

"You sound good though," Amy said.

"Thanks."

Amy didn't have to say it. Lauren knew how she felt and how she sounded when the two parted after she sold the practice. Amy had tried to cheer her up the same way Lauren was trying to get Jake to return to the world. It just hit Lauren that the two of them were similar in that respect. Both she and Jake had had traumas to their lives and both had retreated into themselves. Lauren was by no means over hers, but her clean start in another city was her plan to get her life back on track.

"So what's going on?" Amy cut into her thoughts.

"I need you to get me something and I need it tomorrow."

"That sounds mysterious. What is it?"

"A traditional upper-crust nanny's outfit, complete with straw hat, umbrella and carpetbag."

"What? Why?"

"I've got an idea."

"You're not making any sense," Amy said. There was a question in her tone.

Lauren could practically see her friend staring at the phone as if that would help her decipher what was going on in Lauren's mind.

"I know. Isn't it wonderful?"

"I...I don't know. I wanted you to try something different, not go completely... off course."

"I'm not going off course and I'm not really going on a stage, at least not a Broadway one. I'm going to throw Jake Masters for a loop or make a fool of myself trying."

Amy laughed, her voice a high soprano.

"It's a good thing we live in New York. Here you can get anything you want practically at any time of the day or night."

"Great. Call me and tell me where to meet you."

Talking to Amy always made Lauren feel better. She didn't know what she would have done if Amy hadn't been there to help her through the last year. When Lauren got settled, she'd try to coax Amy out of New York and the two of them could begin again as doctor and nurse.

THE MAIL ARRIVED at the same time every morning. Lauren collected it and separated the circulars and advertisements from the letters. Jake didn't get any personal mail. Correspondence like that probably came through email. She could almost see him hitting the delete key without responding to anything. The letters that arrived were mostly invitations to medical, hospital or corporate functions. He refused them all. If he did open any of the envelopes, their contents often ended up in the trash. If a bill slipped into the pile, he had her send it to his accountant.

When she finished the mail, she found Jake sitting in the great room. He had a book lying open on his knees. Lauren had the feeling it was a prop, there for show only. He was using it to avoid having to speak to her. After two weeks, she was learning his moods and his self-protective instincts. She challenged them at every turn.

"Reading anything interesting?" she asked.

"You wouldn't like it," he said.

He looked at her, but since he'd come down to breakfast and found her wearing a nineteenth century British nanny's outfit, carpetbag at her side, he'd said nothing about her attire. Lauren didn't mention it either. She knew it was eating at him to know why she was dressed that way. She'd let him stew over it until curiosity forced him to ask.

"You have no way of knowing what I like to read. My tastes cover a variety of subjects."

"Anything above a first-grade level?" he mocked.

"Only when absolutely necessary," she joked. She was sure he got her meaning, although his face showed the static emotion of nonchalance. Lauren told herself that he was getting used to her, even if he wouldn't admit it to himself. She guessed he spent most of his time alone except for the people who worked for him. She hadn't seen him talk to anyone since she'd been here. While he treated her with disdain at times, she figured he truly wanted her around.

She'd tested that theory two days ago, by steering clear of him. She stayed in her room or remained in the office for hours. He'd find an excuse to come and see what she was doing. A smile curled her lips when he did this because, whether he wanted it or not, he needed human contact.

"Do you have any friends?" Lauren asked.

Jake's head came up quickly and he looked at her. "Of course I have friends."

"Why don't they come by or call?" She glanced at his cell phone lying on the coffee table. "Why don't you call them? The only people I've seen or heard are here to bring something, clean something or take care of you."

"You don't know that I haven't called my friends."

Lauren gave him her brightest I-know-something-you-don't smile. "You have a lovely voice," she said. "It's deep and thunderous at times. I imagine you could accompany yourself with one hand on that beautiful piano." She glanced at the gleaming yet silent instrument. "But I've never heard you talking on the phone or speaking to anyone when I'm not in the room."

"You listen?" he accused.

"Yes," she said. "Part of my job is to make sure you're all right. If I did hear anything unusual, I'd have to check it out. So far... nothing."

"The truth is most of my friends are doctors and they have very few hours to gab on the phone, much less visit."

Lauren knew that wasn't true, but she held back any comment. Jake was making excuses.

"Will they be at any of those functions you get invitations for? One is a fund-raising ball. You could go there—"

He put up a hand to stop her. "I will not go."

His voice held finality. To punctuate his words, he grabbed his phone as he passed the table and headed out of the room.

Lauren watched him go. His spine was straight and his shoulders back, his steps so stiff she thought he might break.

Anger was an emotion and it was hissing from a crack in Jake's armor.

Lauren smiled.

FIRE HER. IN HIS past life, he'd never put up with someone who talked so much, bullied him and delved into his personal life the way Lauren did. She was relentless. No area appeared to be off-limits to her. She observed everything. How could she know he never talked to any of his friends? She couldn't be monitoring his phone. Jake was extremely tech savvy and he knew his phone was secure.

And the nanny outfit! What was that all about? He'd commented on her not needing to act like a babysitter and here she was in a long dress and boots, her hair done up in an old-fashioned knot.

Nothing about her face was old-fashioned though. The smile was all Lauren's, lively, and never out of place. And all too often Jake found himself getting lost in those wide, expressive eyes of hers. They were her best feature, the one that had him taking her to lunch on the day they met.

He'd retreated to the home gym, but only stood in the room looking at the long wall of mirrors. His grandmother had them installed when his mother was young and wanted to be a dancer. She'd studied for years, but eventually gave up the idea for nursing. The mirrors were still there as a reminder. Jake had the exercise equipment installed when he started working. With such long hours at the hospital, he had little time to travel back and forth to a gym.

He surveyed the room. Everything a modern gym could offer was available to him here. The problem he had was that with only one hand, most of the equipment was little more than giant dust collectors.

The door opened and Lauren stepped in.

"Yes?" he asked. This was the one place in the apartment that she had not yet invaded.

"I wondered if you'd mind if I used the equipment here sometimes?"

"The apartment is yours. With the exception of my rooms, you may use any room you like."

"Thank you," she said quietly and started to back out.

"Lauren," he called.

She looked up. The sun hit her hair again and images of her on the stairs came to him. He felt bad that he'd treated her unkindly. He wasn't that sort of man, at least he hadn't been before the accident. She was here to help him, keep him from being alone. It was unfair that he treated her like an unwelcome guest. The truth was, he enjoyed having someone around to talk to. He hadn't known that until she came, and he was surprised she hadn't run away screaming after the way he behaved.

"Isn't it time for our walk?" he asked.

AND SO THEIR routine began. Except for their daily walks in the park, it was mainly an indoor routine. Lauren looked after everything that required two hands, kept his schedule and sorted his mail. A personal trainer came daily to help Jake exercise in the gym. The housekeeper did the cleaning and oversaw the food deliveries and preparation of meals.

Jake got himself up, showered and dressed. She didn't know how he put his clothes on without help, but he always appeared in his doorway fully dressed and buttoned. She'd volunteered once to tie his sneakers since she noticed the laces were undone. He allowed it, but she felt his discomfort.

"What's it like being a kindergarten teacher?" he asked out of the blue one day as she was massaging his arm. He hadn't asked her to do it, but she'd learned the signs of his pain. Without saying anything, she just began to soothe the aches he felt. At first, he jumped at her touch, but eventually her contact didn't draw that reaction.

"A kindergarten teacher," she said. This was a question she was prepared for. She was a pediatrician and her clientele was primarily under the age of sixteen. She knew how children acted, both when they felt good and when they were ill.

One of Lauren's sisters owned a day care center that also operated a preschool. Kindergarten was the last class for the kids before they began regular school. "It's fun most days. The kids are loud, unruly and eager when they first arrive. Many of them have been to nursery school, so they come knowing a lot. They have to test me as a teacher."

"You should see the look on your face," he said.

Lauren immediately altered her expression. She didn't want to give anything away.

"You obviously like being a teacher. I guess you're planning to do the same thing when you leave here."

"I am," she said, although she felt her guard come up. "What's it like being a surgeon?"

She felt him stiffen, knowing that would be his response.

"Did you always want to go into medicine?"

Lauren stopped massaging his arm. She ran her hand down the length of it, using a nonverbal signal that she was done. She could tell his discomfort had lessened. Moving around him, she sat on a sofa opposite him. Jake looked her directly in the eye. He had a piercing look when he was angry, but that wasn't the expression she saw now.

"Like most kids, I went through a series of professions I wanted to do when I grew up."

Lauren smiled, remembering her own choices. "What were they?"

"Fireman, pilot, truck driver."

"Truck driver?" she laughed.

He smiled. Lauren liked seeing that smile. Lately, she was seeing it more and more. She wondered if it was her presence that brought it out or if he was coming to terms with his injury.

"Did you ever drive a truck?" she asked.

"Once. I was seventeen. At that age, remember, you can do anything."

Lauren didn't acknowledge that.

"I backed it into the side of a building," Jake said. "And there went that career."

Both of them laughed.

"After that I knew I never wanted to do that again. I finished high school and college and went to med school."

"I'm sure there's more to it than that."

"Nothing life altering, although I did meet other med students who were there because they'd lost a loved one and had a calling," he said.

"So, how was it for you?"

He took a moment before answering. "I'd graduated from college and had a job working in economic forecasting. I was bored to death, and during lunch I walked by the med school and went in. I sat down in one of the lecture halls and was so engrossed in the study that I stayed until the class ended and talked to the professor."

"He convinced you to enroll?"

Jake shook his head. "I convinced myself. I felt like this was where I was supposed to be."

Lauren watched him closely. He wasn't looking at her. His eyes were focused somewhere over her shoulder, back in the past to that lecture hall and the man explaining medical procedures.

"I wanted to be that person. I wanted to know how everything worked and how to fix it if it didn't work properly."

"So you did have a calling," she stated.

This time Jake's eyes focused on her. "I had a calling," he said. The surprise in his voice told her the revelation had just come to him.

A moment later, all the progress they'd made in getting Jake to open up was ripped away. Jake glanced down at his arm, then abruptly got up and without a word left the room. Lauren had never been a companion and didn't really know what her patient needed. Not her patient, she corrected herself. She thought they were moving forward. He was talking more, accepting her company and even taking the initiative to join her at times.

Yet when he sank into depression over his arm, she was clueless what to do. She'd made suggestions, but he hadn't taken any of them.

Getting up, she followed him into the kitchen. He appeared to be making coffee.

"Can I help you with something?" she asked.

"I'm perfectly capable of making my own coffee," he snapped.

Lauren nearly jumped at the force of his words. "I'm not the enemy," she said, just as emphatically.

He whipped around. Instinctively, she stepped back. He stared at her for a second, then his shoulders dropped and the fight went out of him.

"I apologize. I didn't mean to shout at you."

She went to the cabinet where he stood and took down the mug he liked to use. Setting it on the counter, she stepped back and spoke softly. "I won't pretend to know what you're feeling. I've never lost the use of any body part. In sports and dancing, my body does what I tell it, adheres to my commands."

"I can't explain it," Jake said.

She didn't expect him to. Lauren watched as he filled the carafe with water and poured it into the coffeemaker. After placing the carafe in the machine and the prepackaged pod in the designed pocket, he closed the lid and hit the brew button. The entire operation was efficiently orchestrated, as if he'd done it all his life.

Lauren had the feeling he was showing her that he was self-sufficient. She no longer felt he was trying to get rid of her, only letting her know that he wasn't a toddler. He could stand on his own without falling down.

JAKE FROWNED WHEN Cal's name and image appeared on his ringing cell phone. Obviously, his only brother wanted to check up on him.

"I'm fine, Cal," Jake said drily, instead of the standard greeting. Cal called each week, always asking about his health. As a structural engineer, Cal was working on a building project in Colorado. Jake had the suspicion that he took the job to force Jake to change from the recluse he'd become.

"Good morning to you too," Cal replied. "How's Lauren? Have you fired her yet?"

"She doesn't work for me. So, as she's reminded me several times, I have no right to fire her."

"I'm sure you tried," Cal laughed.

Jake didn't respond.

"Have you thought of talking to her?"

"Talking to her?" His voice level rose slightly. "She seems to come with batteries that are on perpetual charge mode. I can't get a word in and I've tried." The truth was he did talk to Lauren. If he didn't, she'd force him to answer questions all day.

Cal chuckled. Jake could see the humor, but willed himself to keep his face straight.

"Other than that, how are you doing?"

"I already answered that," Jake said.

"What about the pain in your arm? Is it any better?"

Jake didn't want to admit that he had pain, but Lauren had helped with that.

"She's good at massages," Jake said.

"Massages?"

Jake heard the question in his brother's voice. "My arm, Cal. She massages my arm. Before you left, I told you what she'd done in the restaurant. She's been doing it here too."

"Well, that alone is reason to let her stay. I know how much pain you were in. Is it less now?"

"Yes," he said, not explaining the sharp

decrease he'd experienced in his arm since Lauren put her magic fingers on him.

Caleb didn't say anything for a minute. Jake could hear a muffled sound in the background.

"Sorry, Jake, I have to go now. I'll call you again next week."

"You don't have to keep checking up on me," Jake told him.

"Sure I do. We're brothers and one day we can talk about something other than your arm. Bye."

Jake clicked the end button. He remembered when his conversations with Cal had nothing to do with his arm. The two talked about sports, medicine, their jobs and the places in the world where Cal worked. Cal was always cautious, the planner. Being an engineer suited him, but the brothers had always been close. Jake was the daring one. Cal was more reserved, but they loved each other. They'd had the usual sibling rivalry, but Cal always supported Jake in his choices. Never did he think their conversations would be reduced to Jake's medical needs.

At least now they had Lauren to focus on.

He thought about her and how she'd helped his arm. She had the ability to make his pain go away temporarily. Cal had joked about Lauren's massages, as if there was something between them.

Never, Jake thought.

She wasn't his type and she talked way too much.

"Jake."

There she was.

WALKING IN THE park was an activity Lauren looked forward to. Sometimes they talked and other times they were quiet, but the companionship between them was most evident here. They crossed the street and passed through the gates on a warm July day.

She'd been wearing a different version of the nostalgic nanny outfit for a week, thanks to Amy. Jake eyed her suspiciously. She was bound to draw attention and she wasn't sure he was ready for that. It didn't take long before she was surrounded by children asking who she was pretending to be. Turned out, she was ready for that as she launched into a song and dance, and pretended to pull something magical from her bag. Jake stood to the side, away from her and away from the parents and nannies overseeing the safety of their children.

They recognized that the song she sang was from the remake of the famous musical *Mary Poppins*, and joined in.

She waved goodbye as she rejoined Jake and the kids ran happily back to their parents.

"You're really good with kids," he said.

Lauren couldn't tell Jake that the real reason why, not unless she wanted today to be the last time they saw each other.

"It's the dress and the hat." She glanced up, but all she saw was the brim of the straw hat that went with the costume. "They just want to be loved and happy."

"You don't have any problem wearing that costume out in public in July?"

Lauren checked herself. "Are you kidding? This is New York City. Other than kids, nobody notices. They probably think I'm promoting the play." An updated version was currently on Broadway. "Is it bothering you?"

"I'm a little old to be out with my nanny."

"Well, if anyone says anything, just point

them to me. I'll find something in my magic bag to make them go away."

Lauren was really having fun. The costume was for Jake's benefit, but the kids added a special touch she hadn't counted on.

She clasped his right arm through the sling and wasn't surprised when Jake reacted to the contact.

"What are you doing?" he asked, trying to jerk away from her.

"Nothing different. I usually take your arm when we walk."

"You usually walk on this side." He pointed to the ground with his left hand.

"It makes no difference," she said innocently.

Jake's glare told her she knew it made a difference.

"Jake, you have two arms. So why does it matter which side I walk on? Today, I choose this side."

To drive her point home, she grasped the arm tighter. Checking that there was no sign of pain, she gripped his biceps.

"I see those exercises are working. This arm is a lot stronger," she said, deflecting the subject.

He knew by now that she could be as stubborn as he was and it was best if he just let her have her way. He started walking. He moved fast and Lauren stumbled once before matching his stride.

"Do you think I'll let go if you break into a run?" she asked after they'd maintained the fast walk for three minutes.

Jake stopped. "You know I can do this on my own."

"You've made that very clear. I understand that you're trying to get rid of me. Other than the arm massage, you'd like me to leave for parts unknown."

"Exactly," he said with a smile, only this smile wasn't laced with humor. Bitterness might identify it, nonetheless, it was clear he wanted her gone.

"That's it. You don't want anyone around you. You want to wallow in sorrow and wonder why you? Why did this have to happen to you? You're a surgeon. You fix people. So why take away the one thing that you can do?"

"Careful, Ms. Peterson. You're skating on thin ice."

The stare she gave Jake could melt steel.

She held it for several moments, then dropped his arm and turned around before walking just as fast as he had back toward Central Park West.

It wasn't Jake's fault. He didn't know about her—didn't understand that she'd lost a child.

She reached the apartment in record time. Once in her room, she slammed the door shut and backed up against it. Seconds later, her legs gave out and she slid to the floor.

Lauren couldn't cry. Her eyes were burning but she'd shed all the tears she had a year ago. Her body's trembling was her only outward reaction. She didn't know how long she sat there, her legs curled under her. When she got to her feet, they tingled with the pins-and-needles sensation from sitting in one position for too long.

Jake was wrong. No visible appendage had been taken from her. She'd given it. Free and clear. Without argument or resistance.

THE CITY WAS dark and mysterious outside those massive windows. Night had fallen, and Lauren was alone in the great room. She stared at the horizon in the distance.

Somewhere out there was both danger and adventure. Somewhere a Midwesterner got off a bus in Port Authority and marveled at the sheer number of people, like a human wave, moving through the cavernous building. Lauren had once been one of them.

Looking out the window that faced east, she thought how she loved this room, especially at this time of night. She might have to leave it soon. She and Jake had gotten too close to an argument. She shouldn't feel as if she was forcing him to embrace life when he so clearly wanted to dive into oblivion and stay there. Didn't he have that right?

They weren't friends, but she felt concern for him and his future. It seemed strange for her to be so interested when they'd known each other only a short time. Yet in reality, she *was* a doctor and concern for her fellow man was part of her being. But Jake was more than her "fellow man." She was falling for him.

"What are you doing?"

Lauren jumped. Jake came down the stairs, his left hand sliding along the banister for balance.

When he reached her, she forced a smile,

remembering their earlier encounter in the park. He hadn't appeared for dinner and Lauren had eaten a solitary meal that tasted like sawdust, alone. The food was fine. It was her thoughts that dulled the taste.

"I'm looking at the city."

He glanced through the window and back at her as if there was nothing to see.

"You could smell the roses sometime," she told him.

"We have no roses."

Lauren cut her eyes at him and moved further back into the room. The view was the same, but she was a greater distance from Jake and determined to remain calm and in control of both her emotions and her tongue.

"You know what this room reminds me of?" she asked.

She couldn't see Jake in the dark. He probably raised an eyebrow, but he said nothing. He often did that instead of speaking. She hadn't been around him long enough to know if this action was related to his injury or if he'd always been like that. A third option was that he did it just to perplex her.

"A Hollywood set," she said.

Jake made a sound that said he didn't agree. "I saw a movie once that had a room a lot like this one. A man sat at a piano and played a song, a love song as the screen faded to black."

"I don't watch love stories."

His voice held its familiar gruffness, but Lauren had begun to ignore his tone.

"Do you play the piano?"

She was standing in front of it, a huge concert grand, the frame so shiny she could see her reflection in it on sunny days.

"Not anymore," he said, his voice a low whisper.

"But you did before the accident?" She knew the answer to that question, but she wanted him to know that the mention of the accident was not something that needed to be hidden in a dark room.

"What about dancing?"

"Excuse me?"

"You can't play, but can you dance?"

Again, he stood as if mute.

Lauren went to the CD collection he had and selected one of them. The music wasn't a fast, up-tempo song, but something a little slower. As it began to play, it filled the room with sound. She felt as if it came from every corner of the room.

Going to him, she offered her hand.

"You want to dance?" he asked.

"I do. You have an invitation to a ball. That implies dancing."

"I told you I wasn't going to that ball."

"Going or not going doesn't mean you can't dance."

She took his arm and pulled him forward, placing his hand around her waist. Gently, she began to sway. Jake remained still for a couple of seconds before something appeared to give in him and he joined her. Occasionally she'd brush his right arm as they turned about in a small circle. After a few moments, Lauren forgot about his arm. The night and music carried her. She closed her eyes and let Jake guide her.

The music stopped. Lauren felt an abruptness. She'd overstepped her bounds. She knew it because she liked being this close to Jake. The strength of his left arm as he held her was comforting and safe. She wanted to stay there longer, but the music was no longer giving her a reason to hold on to him.

"You dance very well," she said.

"So do you. I guess you'd like to go to that ball?"

Lauren stepped back. "I'm a companion, remember. I'm not here to date you."

"That didn't answer my question. Would you like to go to the ball?"

Lauren didn't know what to say. *Yes* was on the tip of her tongue. Yet she was unsure of how that answer would affect him.

"You already said you didn't want to go. More emphatically, you said you would not go."

"I've changed my mind. *We'll* go."

CHAPTER FOUR

AMY WAS ALREADY in the restaurant when Lauren arrived. It was near the office where Lauren had had her practice. Amy now worked for the doctors who'd bought the practice. With a wide smile, she waved Lauren over to a table in the back. Still dressed in her nurse's uniform, Amy stood and the two women hugged hello.

They were a contrast to each other. Amy said that accounted for their friendship. Where Lauren was tall with dark brown hair and red highlights all the way to her waist, Amy barely topped off at five feet. Her hair was sandy brown and short to the extreme. Both had dark brown eyes and winning smiles. Amy had dimples that Lauren envied.

"So how are things going?" Amy asked as they sat down.

Lauren knew she didn't want a report of

her relationship with Jake. She was interested in Lauren.

"I'm taking it one day at a time. But I will say that working with Jake is keeping my mind off my problems." Lauren didn't want to dwell on herself. Changing the subject, she asked, "How are things in the office?"

"We're settling in. I had to whip those doctors into shape and now they know who's boss."

Amy was kidding. She was a competent nurse and she suggested better ways of doing things, but never contradicted the doctors' preferences. Often, compromise made the workflow smoother and eased any tension.

"What did Jake think of the costume?"

"It's hard to tell. At first he didn't even acknowledge that I was wearing anything out of the ordinary. Then he told me he wasn't used to going out with a nanny."

"You two are going out?" Amy's voice was hopeful.

"No," Lauren said. "Going out in a literal sense. We go *out* to the park or *out* for a walk."

"Well, here's your new costume," Amy

said, touching the dress bag next to her. "See what he thinks of Princess Lauren."

Lauren partially unzipped the bag and looked at the beautiful ice-blue gown. Small sequins and glass jewels winked at her.

"There was more time to get this one and there's even a crown. I'd love to see Jake Masters's face when you turn up wearing this."

Lauren suddenly laughed.

"What's so funny?" Amy wanted to know.

"I just wondered what Jake's reaction would be if I wore this to the ball."

"Ball? What ball?"

THE APARTMENT WAS silent when Lauren returned from lunch. Jake's town car had picked him up and taken him to an appointment. All Lauren saw on his calendar was the word *dentist*—no name, no phone number or address. And he'd said nothing about how long he'd be gone.

Since it was the first time he'd gone out without her, Lauren used the time to meet Amy and catch up. If he returned before she did, he could be on his own for an hour or two. But when she came in, he was still away.

Lauren took the princess gown to her room and pulled from the bag. The crown lay in the bottom, concealed in a velvet bag. A second bag revealed glass slippers. Well, they were really made of soft plastic, but the effect was the same. Only in a fairy tale could you dance on glass and not cut your feet to shreds.

Lauren pulled the dress up to herself and surveyed its fit in the mirror. Smiling, she danced around the room humming "Ten Minutes Ago." Pushing her shoes off, she wiggled her jeans down and her top off, then slipped the cloud of chiffon over her head. It took a moment to get the zipper up her long back, but she did it. The crown and shoes completed the outfit to the point that she gasped when she saw her reflection. Suddenly, she grinned thinking of the expression on Jake's face if she told him she planned to wear this to the ball.

She twirled a second time to see how the fabric swished about her legs, and then stopped suddenly. Jake had been hurt two years ago. The ball was black-tie. She wondered if he had anything to wear. If he needed to buy or rent a tuxedo, she wouldn't put it past him to wait until it was too late to get one, using it as an excuse to cancel even if it was his idea to go.

Lauren had once loved dressing up and going out. She hadn't done much of it in recent years, but when Jake said they would go to the ball, she was happy. She'd be disappointed if he backed out, but she'd get over it. Jake needed the outing more than she did. She hadn't divorced her friends when her life fell apart. He'd obviously pushed everyone away.

He'd tried pushing her away too. Lauren wasn't going to let that happen.

Leaving her bedroom, she marched to the end of the hall and opened the double doors. The room was empty, full of light and smelled fresh from the housekeeper's recent cleaning. Lauren paused but only briefly before charging straight for a door that was either the bathroom or a closet.

"Closet," she said aloud, then realized the space could double as a New York apartment in some buildings.

The walk-in closet was orderly. Suits, shirts, pants jackets and shoes all had a designated place. She went to the suits, flicking through them as she'd do in the men's department of an upscale store. One by one she checked them and moved on. She'd gotten through only half of them when a voice boomed behind her.

"What are you doing?"

Jake's angry voice thundered in the windowless room. Lauren jumped. Her stomach flopped as her entire body went ice cold, then raging hot.

"Is there something I can help you find or is this just an exploratory operation?"

Lauren turned to face him. "Jake, it's not what it looks like." She put out a hand to steady herself.

He shifted his weight, leaning on his right leg as his left arm grasped one door handle.

"It looks like you're searching for something among my personal things." He raised an eyebrow.

Of course, everything in the space represented his personal things, but Lauren's thoughts went to his clothing.

"I was looking to see if you had a tux." She stopped to swallow. Her throat was drier than sand.

"And you dressed like that to find this

out?" His eyes swept over her from the crown to the glass slippers.

"I thought if you had a tux, it might need to be cleaned and pressed. If you didn't have one, there's time to rent one before the ball."

He gave her an engaging look that didn't convey whether he believed her or not. Lauren withstood his stare, feeling like a thief caught in the act.

Jake moved toward her. She wanted to run, but he stood between her and the open door. She backed up as he approached, knowing the closet would end. As he reached her, he pulled a hanger with a tux from the rack and thrust it into her chest. Reactively, she grabbed it, but he didn't relinquish it. He leaned in close to her. When his face was only an inch from hers, and she could smell the minty scent of mouthwash on his breath, he said, "My dress shirts and cuff links are in the top drawer. Maybe you want to polish them or restitch the tucks on my shirt."

Releasing his hand from the hanger, he turned and walked out of the closet. Lauren held her breath for ten seconds after he vacated the room. Then with a long sigh, she exhaled. Forcing her knees to support her, she returned the tux to its place. She felt like an interloper who'd crossed the line with respect to Jake's personal space. And she had. She should have waited and asked if he had formal attire. But she hadn't and she couldn't put the genie back in the bottle. She had to find him.

Slowly, she left the closet and the bedroom. A wrought-iron railing with intricate grillwork ran the length of the upstairs walkway and down the curved stairway that led to the first level. Where she stood, Lauren had a panoramic view of the downstairs room and the windowed skyline.

Jake wasn't anywhere in sight. She hadn't heard the door open and close, but then she hadn't heard him come in when she was searching through his closet. Checking the walkway, she spied the open door to her bedroom. Rushing to it, she expected to find Jake rifling through her clothes. Yet when she reached the entrance, a smaller version of his rooms, it was totally as she had left it.

Jake was not there.

She admonished herself for thinking he would be petty enough to play tit for tat.

Lauren needed to apologize. She should

never have breached his personal space. She found him in the kitchen. He was staring at the contents of the open refrigerator, but not apparently reaching for anything to eat or drink.

"Jake," she began tentatively. "I apologize. I should have asked you about the tuxedo."

He closed the refrigerator door. The soft whoosh that usually accompanied the action sounded more like a hard thump.

"If you'd like to cancel going to the ball, I fully understand."

He said nothing, making her feel even worse than she already did.

"If you'd like me to leave, I'll go. What I did was unforgivable. I'll call your brother and—"

"We're going," he interrupted, his movement rapid as he passed her and walked out of the kitchen with the abruptness that he did everything. Lauren didn't understand. This was what he wanted. He had the perfect excuse to get rid of her. Why hadn't he?

Why did he not only forgive her lapse in judgement, but was still taking her to the ball? She put her hand to her head, realizing she was getting a headache. Her fingers came in contact with the crown. She certainly didn't feel like a princess, more like a witch.

JAKE CLOSED THE door to his bedroom. The closet was as neat as it was when he left it earlier in the day. Lauren had replaced the tux in exactly the same spot where he'd found it. And he'd acted like a louse. It was a surprise finding her in his closet. At first he hadn't realized who it was. Then she turned and the dress, the crown, even the surprise on her face made him angry with himself. Angry that the effect of seeing her dressed like that churned up memories in him of their dance the other night and an awareness of her that he didn't want.

He'd lashed out in anger, made even worse when he stood so close to her that he could have kissed her. He wanted to kiss her. But fear was in her eyes. He knew part of it was guilt because of how she'd been found out, but he caused the other part.

She'd come in the kitchen and given him a solution to the problem of his growing feelings for her. Why didn't he take it? He'd told her that he didn't need her, didn't need a babysitter, yet when he had the perfect opportunity to act on his wishes, he caved.

She'd gone from a nanny to a princess. Memories of them dancing in the dark, swaying slowly to the music, came to him. He hadn't danced since before he was hurt, yet with her, with Lauren he'd circled the room unaware of his unused arm. She made him feel like he could do anything. He teetered on anger that she made him forget and the fact that no matter what, when reality set in, his arm would never be as it once was.

A soft knock came at the door. Jake was standing in the middle of the room. There was no one else in the apartment. It had to be Lauren at the door.

"It's open," he said.

The lock mechanism turned silently and the door swung inward. Jake forced himself not to gasp at the sight of a princess fully bathed in sunlight. She stood on the outside of the threshold.

"You asked for a late lunch," she said.

"My dental appointment," he reminded himself. The numb sensation from the dental work had worn off and he hadn't even noticed.

"It's here."

Lauren turned to leave. Jake wasn't sure if she was going to her rooms or not, but he didn't want her to go.

"If it would please, her highness—" he called.

"Just Lauren will do," she said.

"Well, *Lauren*, will you join me for lunch?"

"I've already eaten," she said. "But I will join you for a soft drink."

They walked to the kitchen, where Lauren had deposited the bag containing his lunch. It was meat loaf with gravy and mashed potatoes, his favorite. He opened the package, got a plate from the cabinet and started filling it with the food.

"There's enough for two," he said to Lauren.

She shook her head. "Just the drink."

Jake went to the refrigerator and pulled out a bottle of water and a soft drink. He set them in front of her, along with a glass. She reached for the soft drink and twisted the top off.

She got up and went to the refrigerator. The automatic ice maker plopped cubes into her glass. She came back at the same time he sat down.

"How long are we going to be subjected to this version of a poor urchin girl changed into a princess?"

"I don't know. I have three gowns."

"Well, you can play the princess, but don't expect me to take on the role of prince."

She looked away, fiddling with her glass. "If a poor urchin girl can change into a princess, maybe a crotchety old man can turn into a charming prince."

"Don't count on it."

"Maybe I'll wear one of the dresses to the ball." She stopped and touched the crown perched on her head. "And the tiara."

Jake dropped the fork full of mashed potatoes. It slipped off the table, catching on his pant leg before plopping to the floor.

Lauren put a hand up and snickered. It turned into a small laugh that grew and grew. She closed her eyes as the laugh burst into full-blown mirth. Tears gathered at the corners of her eyes. She pointed at him, but she was laughing so hard, she could say nothing.

"It isn't that funny," he told her.

"You…" she gasped. "You…" Laughter claimed her. She couldn't talk. "Your…face… You have no idea."

THE BUZZING SOUND was irritating. Jake tried to ignore it, hoping it would go away, but it persisted. Then he realized it was his phone. He'd set it on silent and the buzz was the vibration against the bedside table. Reaching for it, he wondered who was calling at this hour. The sun couldn't be up yet. His room had blackout shades, so there was no ambient light filtering through the sides of the windows.

Swiping his thumb across the answer button, he put the phone to his ear.

"This better be good," he said.

"Why? Are you in bed with someone?"

Jake sat up straight and checked the covers beside him.

"Cal?" he questioned.

"Good morning." Jake recognized his brother's voice.

"Is everything all right?" Jake asked. Rarely did they speak this early.

"I'm calling to see how things are going with you."

"With me and the princess?"

Who?"

Jake mentally shook himself. Cal knew nothing about Lauren and her costume changes.

"Is that code for you acting like a prince?"

"Not in the least," Jake replied.

"So how is it going with Lauren?"

"She's surprising," he said. It was the truth. He never knew what she was going to say or do. When she first appeared in that nanny outfit, he didn't say a word about it. Instead of forcing him to comment, she just acted as if there was nothing unusual about the way she was dressed.

"Surprising, how?"

Jake wouldn't mention the costumes. He looked forward to seeing what she would wear next. And like she said, it was New York. No one looked more than twice at what she wore on the street. It didn't seem to bother her and at times she entertained kids, providing a few moments of fun for them. It was an unusual, but kind thing to do. Compassionate, even.

Jake had the feeling that the stories and dance steps weren't for the kids, but for him.

She was trying to tell him something. To get his attention. She didn't know it, but she already had it.

"My arm is usually free of pain after she massages it." Jake finally answered his brother's question.

"How often have you threatened to fire her?" He heard the laughter in Cal's voice.

"Daily, but you know her response."

"She doesn't work for you, but for me," Cal said.

"Exactly."

"Do me a favor." Cal's voice turned serious. "Give her a chance for more than your arm."

"What do you mean?" he asked. Jake's mind went to them dancing in the dark. How she felt in his arms and how he loved holding her.

"I mean talk to her, get to know her, don't just issue orders."

"I tried that. It didn't go so well."

Cal gave a short laugh. "Sounds like she might be a match for you."

"Not a match," he said. "She's temporary, remember."

"Yeah, has she said when she's leaving?"

"No." Jake was taken aback by the reminder. She hadn't been there that long, but she'd insinuated herself into his routine. He liked having her around. She often anticipated his wishes before he knew what they were. She was friendly with the housekeeper and the other tradespeople who came to the apartment. Jake could often hear her laughing when someone else was there.

Cal was quiet for a moment and Jake recognized the silence. His brother hadn't called just to inquire about his health.

"What is it, Cal?" he asked.

Cal sighed. "I know it's an old argument, but hear me out."

Jake waited for him to continue.

"You've withdrawn from the world. As long as Lauren is there, try some outings that aren't related to your injury. Go to a movie or out to dinner, and I don't mean sit in the media room and watch the big screen. Leave the apartment. Get used to being in the world, not looking at it from the top floor of the apartment."

Cal had no idea how many times Lauren had gotten him out of the apartment. "You're in luck, Cal. Lauren and I go out every day."

"You do?"

"Lauren is a real taskmaster. She gets what she wants. You couldn't have picked a better companion."

"So you like her?"

"Let's not go that far. Let's just say I haven't changed the lock on the front door."

This time Cal's laugh was genuine. "Well, that's a start."

"So, how's it going with you? Anyone you're spending time with?"

Jake had felt a little guilty for taking so much of his brother's attention. After the accident, Cal had endured Jake's anger and spent a lot of time trying to help him. That included giving up his social life so Jake wouldn't be alone.

Cal had to be on the ground when it came time to consult on a project and when the opportunity came for him to lead a team in Colorado, Jake agreed he should go. Cal was adamant that he wouldn't leave Jake alone. And that's how Lauren had come into his life. Jake smiled despite himself.

"No, there is no one special out here. I work a lot. There's little time for socializing."

Jake thought it ironic that the person who was always preaching to him to be more social had no social life. And Jake did.

At least the shadow of one.

JAKE PRESSED THE end button on his phone and dropped it on the bed. Pushing the covers aside, he swung his feet to the floor to propel himself to stand. The phone slipped to the floor and Jake instinctively reached for it with his right arm, but the arm didn't move.

He cursed and stood up, leaving the phone where it lay as he headed for the shower. Minutes later water pelted against his skin. He scrubbed himself with the extralong brush that worked better than a washcloth. It reached all the way down his back. When he'd finished, he stood under the slicing water. The phone call hadn't set well with him.

He wasn't falling for Lauren. She was here only to keep him company. He clamped a hand on his right shoulder. Nothing flowed through him, not the warmth of her hands, not the magic that took the pain away whenever her fingers kneaded his flesh. Unceremoniously, he snapped the shower off.

Ten minutes later, he walked into the kitchen to find his beaming princess standing at the sink. The sight of her hit him like a lightning bolt. Jake's mouth went dry and he could hardly move for several seconds.

"What are you planning to wear next time? A mermaid costume?" Jake asked. "I'm looking forward to seeing that. Not sure how you'll get around with a tail, though. Especially when we're walking in the park."

"Mermaids only live in the sea," she told him. "If I did that, I'd have to take you with me and you don't like the water."

Throwing the dish towel she was holding into the sink, she glared at him.

What was wrong with him? How she dressed wasn't the issue. He actually enjoyed the surprises she threw his way. Everything had been fine a minute ago. It was Cal who put the idea in his head that he might be having feelings for Lauren.

He didn't.

She was amusing and he liked talking to her. He enjoyed their dance together, but other than that there was nothing between them. And there would be nothing between them. She'd made it clear that she was there on only a temporary basis. Getting involved with him could deter her plans. And she wasn't a person to let anything get in the way of what she wanted. That much he knew for certain.

"What happened between last night and this morning?" she asked. "Something has set you off and you're taking it out on me."

"So you're a psychologist now?"

"I don't need to be a psychologist to see that you're ready for a fight. You've been trying to wear me down. Since you couldn't fire me, you've been trying to get me to quit."

"I didn't want another nurse."

"I'm not a nurse, and I haven't tried to be one," she said. "But you're not equipped to take care of yourself. You can't even button your shirt. That's why you wear those pullovers. How you get in them alone is beyond me."

Jake knew she said that to get a rise out of him.

"I can button my shirt," he shouted. "And I'm well aware of how helpless I am."

"You're not helpless," she said, her volume equal to his. "At least not in the way you want to believe. You're capable of thousands of tasks."

"And not one of them allows me to tie my shoes."

"Big deal. Buy shoes that don't have ties."

They stared at each other like two warring enemies.

"You can do what you want to do," she said.

"How about surgery. Can I do that?"

"No." Some of the fight seemed to leave her. "But if you have to, you can still use all the medical training you have."

"How?"

"Someone taught you how to be a surgeon. You didn't pop out of the womb with a scalpel in one hand and a wealth of knowledge on the human body inside your head."

"Are you again suggesting I teach?" He grunted instead of laughing. "That old adage. I've gotten to the point where I can't do, so I can teach."

"It's an important profession, one that is both revered and needed. However, I only said you are not helpless. But I take that back. You are helpless. Anyone who can't see his own value and for two years has wallowed in self-pity is helpless."

"I don't need this from you or anyone else. You can leave and don't come back again. You're fired."

"You can't fire me." She pointed to her chest. "I can quit, but it was your brother who hired me, remember? Who gave me the skinny on you and your outbursts. And if I go, it'll be on my terms, not those of someone who's ranting and acting as if he were helpless."

They'd had this argument before. Would it ever end?

CHAPTER FIVE

WITH ONE LONG glance at Jake, Lauren turned and left the room. She was angry when she closed the door behind her. For several minutes she stood there, remembering their argument and wishing it had gone another way.

Jake was hurting. She shouldn't have said those things to him, yet they needed to be said. Not necessarily in that way. But Lauren knew if he didn't confront his fear, he'd never be any good. She was a pediatrician and he was acting like a child. She could help him. Of course, it would go faster if he would admit his problem and begin to heal.

She couldn't tell him she was a doctor. Even without his brother present that would be grounds for dismissal. But despite how the day had gone, she had to go on tomorrow. When this was finally over, she'd find a new place to live and begin her new practice. She could put Jake Masters out of her mind and get on with her life. She could see now that his attack had changed him, robbed him of all the compassion and trust he must have formerly possessed.

She only hoped there was a way of getting those things back.

Lauren and Jake bumped around each other for the next three days. She'd walk into a room and he'd leave it. He refused to go to the park with her. They exchanged few words, more grunts than any recognizable language. The only thing Jake said directly to her was he thought she should cut short her time with him and begin her new life.

Her heart dropped. They'd had heated encounters before and they always got past them. This time it felt as if he disliked her so much, he really didn't want her around. The pain of his words struck her like a knife to the heart. She had thought he was thawing, but now he'd erected a wall and the friendship she had believed they were building had ended. They were back to being the enemies they were on the first day she'd arrived at the apartment.

On the morning of the fourth day of war,

Lauren woke with a new resolve. She dressed as a ballerina thanks to Amy's resourcefulness. Lauren was completely in white: tutu, stockings and ballet slippers. She didn't even consider getting pointe shoes. It had been decades since she took ballet and her toes were no longer prepared for the pressure of her body weight balanced on them.

She was in the great room near the piano practicing her pirouette when she heard a laugh from above. Spinning around, she saw Jake on the upstairs walkway.

"Do you know how ridiculous you look?" he asked.

Lauren could almost hear the ice breaking. The outfit had done its job. He couldn't go back to grunts now. Well, he could, but their impact wouldn't be the same.

"And how are you today?" she asked. She waited, wondering if he was going to be the same angry man he'd been for the last several days.

He came down the stairs, the smile on his face was at her expense, but she was so used to him showing no reaction to her outfits that she considered it a step forward.

"I'm not the one who's going to look ridiculous even on the streets of New York."

"All eyes will be on me and not you," she said.

Lauren never thought she'd be bold or daring enough to appear in public dressed as various characters. But since Jake came into her universe, she'd thought and done things that were not part of her usual behavior.

The old-fashioned nanny outfit came to mind. It should have been the only one. She assumed it would force Jake to change and the relationship between them would improve. When they went outside, it would focus attention on Lauren and not on Jake's arm. Yet Jake had proved to be more stubborn than she anticipated. The ballerina had unleashed a greater response from him. She didn't know how long it would last. Would he suddenly revert to his earlier uncommunicative self?

Lauren couldn't determine what his reaction would be, but she had another plan. And she was sure he wasn't going to like it.

"About the ball," she started.

He said nothing, but looked her straight in the eye.

"Is it still on the calendar?"

"What if I say no?" he asked.

She took two steps toward him. "Then I'll organize a party here, inviting a few of your colleagues." Of course, she'd invite only people who didn't know her. Since she was a pediatrician, they didn't travel in the same medical circles.

"I won't attend it."

"Then I'll remove the lock from your door and bring the entire party to your bedroom. Your choice."

"You would, wouldn't you?"

"Test me on it."

Despite what she was wearing, she was dead serious. "You've been hiding here long enough. If you don't want to be helpless all your life, you have to let people in. These are your friends. They were before the accident and they still are. They didn't change. You did."

"Okay."

"Okay, what?" she asked.

"I only said what *if* I say no."

"So your answer is yes?"

"You're relentless. You know that?"

Lauren smiled. "That's the best thing you've ever said to me."

LAUREN SHOPPED FOR several days before the ball. The idea of a party had her rushing around. She wanted the perfect dress and it had been a long while since she thought of dressing up for anything more than a medical convention. There would be a lot of medical professionals in attendance, but she was there only for Jake's welfare and the pleasure of proving to him that spending time with his colleagues would be beneficial.

She had several evening gowns that would be appropriate, but they were packed away in storage.

The gown she settled on was a regal purple with a high neck in the front. The back plunged into a deep V. She wore her hair up in a mass of curls. Her jewelry consisted of pearl earrings and a pearl necklace that draped down her back.

Jake appeared at the top of the stairs. Lauren looked up and her breath caught in her throat. Both her heart and her stomach dropped at the sight of him. She'd never seen him in anything other than casual clothes. Wearing the tux, he was devastatingly handsome. The sling he usually wore to hold his right arm was gone.

Wow was the word that came to mind, but her voice was gone and she uttered nothing.

"You look amazing," he said, stepping off the last rung.

"So do you." Her voice sounded low and breathy, like some television actress seeing her gorgeous leading man for the first time.

A soft knock on the door interrupted them.

"That would be the driver," Jake said.

The party was in full swing when they arrived. The ballroom, done in blue and white, was beautifully appointed. Lauren took Jake's right arm. Immediately, his former colleagues greeted him. Whenever one of them forgot and offered to shake hands, Lauren took the hand and introduced herself. She found this action left no one embarrassed. She spotted no clues from Jake that he was tired, or that he wanted to leave. He seemed to be having a good time. After the first half hour, Lauren left him to to catch up with his old friends.

Never far away, she gave him space and mingled among the medical professionals, eavesdropping on their conversations. When invited to join them, she told them she wasn't a surgeon, leaving out that she understood most of the talk that was going on.

Finally the program began, followed by dinner and dancing.

"Are you all right?" she asked Jake when the music started. "Would you like to leave?"

"I believe you wanted to dance," he told her.

He stood up and offered her his hand. Lauren took it and they walked to the dance floor. She turned in his arms the way she'd done in the apartment, taking his right elbow as his left hand slipped around her waist and his right hand rested on her shoulder. They started to circle the floor, moving slowly so his hand wouldn't slip.

"I'll lead," she said, since their positions were reversed.

"Of course. I'm sure you're used to leading," he whispered against her ear.

She heard the humor in his voice and smiled and they swayed together. Checking the crowd, she observed that no one was taking note of them. She relaxed in his arms and let the music and the night unfold.

Later, they sat at their table, talking amicably, when they were joined by someone Jake knew.

"Jake, good to see you." A tall young man with brown hair, glasses and clear blue eyes stood before them. He offered Jake his hand, the gesture so automatic that it was done without thought.

Lauren stepped in, so to speak, and shook his hand.

"Hello, I'm Lauren, Dr. Masters's assistant."

"Lauren, this is Dr. Douglas Faris. He's a trauma surgeon also."

"Good to meet you," he said. "And please call me Doug."

"Did you two work together?" Lauren asked.

"Yes, and I want him to come back and work with me again."

"I don't see how I can be much help," Jake said. "Surgery requires two hands. And trauma is an animal in itself. It requires strength and quick action."

A couple of other doctors came over and the conversation veered off in different directions. Lauren willingly stepped back, keeping out of the conversations on medicine. She didn't want to show her hand and knew it could easily happen if she had an opinion on something that someone else was saying.

A woman came up to her near the table where they were seated for the evening.

"Lauren, right?" she asked.

Lauren nodded.

"I'm Paula Ingraham. A colleague of Jake's. How's he really doing?" she asked.

"Very well," she said. Even though Jake wasn't her patient, discussing a person's medical information was taboo.

"I've tried to call him several times, but he never returns my messages."

Lauren was grateful for that bit of information. "He's been dealing with his brother being away and his circumstances."

She tried to be as vague as possible. Cal left only a few weeks ago and Jake had been in the apartment long enough to know it blindfolded.

"So what exactly do you *do* for him?" Paula asked.

She was direct and Lauren figured she'd already decided on the answer.

"I keep him safe," she said.

"Does that include dressing him and—"

"He's mastered that on his own," Lauren interrupted. "Look, I'm his assistant, not his lover," Lauren told her.

"I didn't mean—"

"I know exactly what you mean. So to clear your mind, his brother hired me to make sure Jake adhered to his schedule while he was away, and if he needed any help someone would be there. I live in the apartment. I have my own rooms and we don't share. Anything else you want to know?"

"I didn't intend to pry."

"Then I apologize. Excuse me."

Lauren left her. She knew exactly what the woman intended. She was attracted to Jake and Lauren appeared to be her competition. Not only did she live at the same address as Jake, but she got to see him on a daily basis. According to Dr. Ingraham, he didn't return her phone calls. Maybe that should tell her something.

Lauren moved back to where Jake was engaged in conversation with a trio of doctors. He reached for her hand when she got close enough. Lauren felt her blood pressure returning to normal.

"Have you met everyone?" Jake asked, indicating the doctors in front of him.

Lauren nodded. "I thought we might dance," she said.

"That's a wonderful idea."

"Jake, think about what we said," a salt-and-pepper-haired doctor name Wilford Styles said. "We'd love to have you back with us."

"I'll think about it," he responded, then led Lauren to the floor. "Having a good time?" he asked when he turned her into his arms.

"It's better now," she said.

"What did she say?" he asked.

"Who?"

"I saw you talking to Paula. Did she upset you?"

"It's nothing," Lauren said. She felt as if the conversation was moot. She was dancing with Jake and she felt light in his arms.

"I want to know," he said.

"All right." She reviewed the conversation. "Apparently, she has designs on you and she sees me as competition."

"I'm not interested in Dr. Ingram."

Lauren smiled. "It doesn't matter if it's one-sided. She still thinks she has a chance."

"Let's show her she doesn't."

Jake put his left hand under her hair and pulled her close to his shoulder. They danced around the floor that way. Lauren felt everyone was watching them. Her concern was no longer about Dr. Paula Ingram, but about the man holding her. His aftershave made her heady and both the arm pressed at her back and the one between them had her feeling as if they were in their own magic world.

Jake kissed the side of her face, just where her hairline met her cheek. While Lauren couldn't see Paula Ingram, she was sure Jake had waited until she was in view before kissing her. Lauren leaned back, knowing the emotions coursing through her would quickly race out of control if she remained where she was. The movement proved a mistake. When she looked at Jake, his eyes were filled with desire and his mouth was only a breath away from hers.

IT WAS GLORIOUS, she thought hours later as they returned to Central Park West. Lauren slipped out of her shoes just inside the door.

"Did you have a good time?" Jake asked.

"I really felt like an actual princess," she said. "Even if I wasn't wearing my gown and crown."

They walked farther into the apartment, going to the sofa and sitting down. Jake pulled his tie loose and with one hand unbuttoned the top button on his shirt.

"I danced and danced. And I didn't have to flee at midnight or watch the town car turn into a pumpkin," Lauren said, almost cheering when she noticed Jake smile.

He looked at her and Lauren felt bathed in warmth. She should turn away, but she liked the way he looked at her. They weren't enemies now. They were friends, companions.

"What about you?" She could see he seemed tired. "You appeared to enjoy talking with your friends."

"It was grueling," he said.

"Liar. I saw you smiling and talking medical techniques and new procedures with a bunch of doctors." She was careful to keep her words in laymen's terms.

"It was interesting to hear about the progress that's happened in the last few years."

He'd once been part of that progress, she knew. He missed it. Even if he didn't say it out loud, she could hear it in his tone.

"And what about Paula Ingraham? I thought she was going to tip you over at one point. She held on to your arm so tightly." After her conversation with Paula, she'd managed to avoid the surgeon for the rest of the night. It was obvious Dr. Ingraham wanted more from her former colleague.

"Jealous?" Jake asked, a wry smile curving his lips.

The question threw Lauren. She *was* jealous. "Slightly," she admitted, waiting a moment to see his reaction. "She got you to smile in only five minutes. It took me three days."

"There's nothing there," he said. "We mostly talked about the hospital, people we both know."

She felt he was refusing to admit that he enjoyed mingling in his old community, even with Paula.

"I heard someone ask you about consulting."

He nodded, without comment.

"Are you going to do it?"

"I told him I'd give it some thought."

"But you're not going to?" Lauren asked.

"I didn't say that."

"You don't have to," she told him. "It's obvious from every pore in your body."

"You think it's something I should do?" he stated.

"I think you're healthy. You have a sound mind. And deep down, I think you want to use it. But pride holds you back. You anticipate how you think people will react to your arm."

"I'm usually right," he said matter-of-factly.

"That might be, but when you begin to speak, no one thinks of anything except the intelligence you share. I cannot tell you what to do. You have to decide what you want your life to be."

He grunted, making a sound that said nothing.

"What?" she asked.

"You sound like Cal. He says I should accept what I can't change and use what I have, meaning my brain, to make it happen."

"Good advice," Lauren agreed.

"That's why he hired you."

"I don't understand," she said.

"Cal took that job in Denver to force me to make a decision. He didn't want me to be here alone, so he hired you to replace him. A stranger who would do what Cal was doing, but from a different perspective."

"Only I'm not doing what Cal did. I'm getting you up and out even against your wishes," she said.

"Not exactly against my wishes."

Lauren smiled. She was making progress.

"Secretly, I think you like it. It's just that you also like being a grump."

"I am not a grump," he contradicted.

THE END OF the ball marked an end to the fairy-tale costumes. Lauren dressed in regular clothes. It was evident three days later. Jake noticed she'd worn only street clothes, shirts and pants or shorts and tops. He admitted he missed the different outfits. He never knew what she would come up with next, still, her own personality came through regardless of her chosen dress.

There was another change, and this one

he'd decided on. He *would* consult. With the computer facilities he had, he didn't need to be present in the hospital. At other times, he'd try his hand at medical writing. In school he'd gotten good grades in English and didn't have a problem organizing his thoughts. There were a lot of procedures he and his former team developed that needed to be put down on paper and completely described. He could do that.

He should thank Lauren for suggesting it, even though he'd been resistant. He might well never get the use of his arm back. He might never enter an operating room as a surgeon again. But he was a young man. He was in his thirties. Forty or fifty years lay before him. He couldn't see himself continuing to get up and rattle around this apartment doing nothing for the next five decades.

It was a stark realization. What was he going to do with his life? The one he'd had was gone and he had to come to terms with that. He went into the office. Lauren wasn't there. She wasn't in the apartment and had not told him where she was going. He sighed, realizing he missed her. Several boxes addressed to him arrived that morning and were sitting in the corner. He'd ordered them the day after the ball and until now they'd remained unopened.

Juggling them with one arm, he took them to his bedroom and installed a video conferencing system on a table his grandmother had told him was a family heirloom. He'd never thought much about it, but because of her, he didn't move it or use it often. Now it held the face-to-face communication unit and a laptop on which he installed a voice recognition program.

Trying it out for the first time was awkward. He wasn't used to hearing himself speak to a machine. And he'd never dictated before. He'd given orders, but that was like staccato speech. Sentences were clipped or fragmented and medical code was used to tell the nurses what he wanted done. This required a new style of speaking. But for Lauren's sake, he'd try it.

He heard the apartment door open and close, and his heart raced a little. She was back.

"Jake," she called.

He left the room and looked over the ban-

ister. She looked up at him. The wind had
ruffled her hair, and her face glowed.

"Let's go for a drive."

CHAPTER SIX

JAKE HAD A CAR. Lauren had casually spoken to the doorman and learned that Jake maintained a car and a parking space nearby. It hadn't been used since his accident, but it was still there.

Instead of walking the same route through the park every day, they would have a greater reach to the outside world with a car.

"Where?"

"Jake, you have a car. Let's take it out for a spin."

"I haven't… I mean it hasn't been used in a while. It probably won't run."

"Let's go see. I'll drop these packages and we'll get lunch—in New Jersey."

He opened his mouth to refuse, but Lauren was still talking.

"Meet you in five minutes. Bring the keys."

She didn't wait to see what he said or did. She wasn't giving him a choice. Five minutes later, he was standing by the door. She rushed toward him.

"Do you have a valid driver's license?" he asked.

"I do. I've got my car parked in a lot not far from here. But I don't drive that often," she told him.

"How long has it been?"

She smiled. "Are you afraid I'll have an accident?"

"It's a possibility."

"A few weeks ago. I went to an interview." She left it at that.

Lauren raised her hand for the keys. Jake took his time, but he passed them over. She reached for both the keys and his hand as she led him out of the apartment.

She should have known the car would be a sporty model. Jake led her to a bright yellow Mercedes. He opened his own door and got in, but he couldn't pull it closed. Lauren did so, then clicked the button to open the trunk before getting behind the wheel, slipping onto a seat that was as smooth and soft as butter.

"What did you put in the trunk?"

"My sweater and jacket. My parents

taught me to always take something in case the weather changed."

The engine fired on the first try. She smiled and put the car in gear. It drove like a dream.

"Enjoying yourself?" Jake asked after several minutes. He seemed to like watching her.

"It handles like it knows what I want to do. All I have to do is think it and the car responds."

"Almost," he said with a smile.

Lauren was sure he hadn't intended for her to see it. She negotiated the streets of Manhattan, then took the tunnel into New Jersey. Once there, Lauren opted for the turnpike. Although the speed limit was sixty-five, she exceeded it by fifteen miles and hardly felt any pull on the car.

"I think you should slow down," Jake said. "Not only is the car unfamiliar to you, but you will get pulled over by the police."

"It's almost worth it," Lauren said, but she slowed down anyway. She drove past exit after exit until they were close to Princeton.

"Aren't we going to stop for lunch?" Jake finally asked.

"Soon," she said.

"I wonder how long you would keep driving if this was a convertible."

"I've never driven a convertible. My first car was an old Chevy that was handed down to me. I was forever fixing it since it was always breaking down."

"A mechanic in our presence," he teased.

Lauren was loving this. She hoped this Jake would remain as the dominant personality. He was funny, playful and good to be around. Lauren saw her exit. She took a side road that was wide, but not heavily trafficked. Ten minutes later she slowed and turned into a public park.

"Here?" Jake questioned. "We're having lunch here?"

"We're having a picnic."

She parked, cut the engine and got out. Again she opened the trunk and instead of pulling out a sweater and jacket, she took out the picnic basket and a blanket.

"How'd you do that?" He indicated the picnic basket.

"I ordered it and the doorman put it in the parking garage. When I opened the car, I stored it in the trunk along with my sweater and jacket."

After choosing a place close to the pond, Lauren spread the blanket and sat down. Jake joined her. Together they put out the food.

"When was the last time you went on a picnic?" she asked.

"I don't remember."

"It was with her, right?"

"Her?"

"Yes, the woman who you don't mention. And before you ask, Caleb said nothing about a woman, girlfriend, fiancée, friend or even a person of interest."

"So, why do you think there was someone?"

"Because I wasn't born yesterday and I recognize the signs if not the photo."

His head came up and he stared at her. Lauren hoped she wasn't changing his mood, forcing him back into the sullen Jake.

"I found it on the shelves behind the piano. I was looking at some music and a photo slipped from between the pages."

"The last picnic wasn't with her. It was with a patient, a seventeen-year-old girl with a heart transplant that was rejecting. She told me she had only one wish before she died."

Lauren stopped moving and sat back on her heels.

"She wanted to feel the sun on her face. The nurses organized a picnic on the hospital grounds. There's an inner courtyard designed to look like a park."

"You took her there?"

He nodded. "She laughed and cried, ate a little. She told us stories about her life. It was a happy day."

"But it was sad for you." Lauren knew the memory wasn't good. "Tell me the last picnic you attended where you were happy."

"It was a beach picnic. We were in Florida on the gulf side. The sun was hot, the water warm. Cal was there. We spent the entire day and part of the night. We had food and music, swimming races and sailing. After the sun set, we had a fire on the beach. Sitting around it, we told ghost stories."

"That sounds like fun."

Lauren was dying to ask if she was there, the woman in the photo, but held her tongue. She recognized Jake. Cal had told her how athletic he was, how he once did extreme sports before going to med school. Sailing and swimming were two things that would excite him.

The day passed quietly. While they ate, Lauren told him about her life, keeping to the script of the kindergarten teacher. She told him about her family and things she and her sisters had done as kids and teenagers. Eventually, she and Jake lapsed into a companionable silence.

"What are you going to do when you leave here?" Jake asked after a while. "Are you going back to teaching kids?"

"Probably. I don't know for sure." Lauren shook her head and looked toward the sky to prevent Jake from seeing there was something about his question that touched her. "What about you? When I leave are you going to retreat into your bedroom and only come out to eat?"

He chuckled. "I think I'm past that."

Lauren looked back quickly, her smile wide. Her hand was on his right arm before she thought about it. "Glad to hear it."

He smiled at her and Lauren started to move her hand, but Jake clasped it in place. Their eyes met and held. Lauren's brain shouted at herself to look away, move her hand, but something else inside her wouldn't let it happen. She didn't know how long they stared at each other. The bond that held them suspended, pulled them closer to one another. Lauren's eyes were closing when she realized what was happening. He was going to kiss her. She wanted him to kiss her. But she pulled away, sat up straight.

"I'm sorry," she said. "I'm your companion and I should have remembered that."

Jake cleared his throat, but didn't say anything. She saw his shoulders rise and fall as he took a long breath.

"Maybe we should leave," he suggested.

It was late afternoon, time to return to the city. Time to return to reality.

Once everything was packed in the car, Lauren held the keys out to Jake. He looked at them and then at her as if the world was about to end.

"No," he said emphatically. "I haven't driven since the accident."

"Yet you keep a valid driver's license," she teased, trying to lighten the mood.

"Identification," he said. "I need it to get on planes."

"You haven't been on a plane since you returned from Paris."

"I guess Cal told you everything there is to know about me."

"He didn't have to. I can tell a lot of things about you from your attitude."

"Then you should know that driving is one of the things that's off-limits to me," he said.

"This parking area is huge and there are no other cars around." Going to him, she took his arm, tugging him toward the driver's side of the low sporty model.

The parking lot was empty of cars except for Jake's. It was a workday. The lunchtime crowd didn't get out this far and it was well past four o'clock.

"We should go," Jake said. "As it is we're going to get caught in the rush-hour traffic."

"I think you should drive." Lauren said it nonchalantly as if she was offering him a cookie. She grabbed the keys and dangled them in front of him. Jake stepped back as if she had a snake in her hand.

"I can't drive."

"Why not?"

He looked perplexed, as if she was being facetious.

"You haven't been away from the wheel that long. You wouldn't have forgotten how in a couple of years. If your medical knowledge is still there, then so is your ability to drive."

"One of those has nothing to do with the other." He glanced at his arm.

"Don't try that." Lauren cut him off. "If you don't want a skill to atrophy, then you need the practice. And what better place to try than here?"

Lauren opened her arms to encompass the deserted area.

"Don't you want to try?" She whispered the words, giving him an option she knew he wanted. "Don't you want some independence? If you can drive yourself, you can go where you want without a companion." She let her voice rise a little at the end.

Jake said nothing. Lauren could tell he was thinking about it. She waved the keys close to his face.

"Don't do that," he said.

"Why not?" Lauren continued waving the keys. She stepped closer to Jake, baiting him. She knew she had him when he stopped backing up. Her final step had her nearly bumping into him.

"Come on, give it a try. What do you have to lose?"

Jake looked down at her. With a sigh, he took the keys.

Lauren ran around and slipped into the passenger seat. "It's a very powerful car," she told him. "Be careful, the owner is a real grouch. He'll probably have you drawn and quartered if you hit a blade of grass."

Jake cut his eyes at her, but accepted the criticism with a smile. He pressed the start button. The car purred to life. Lauren noticed the slight smile of satisfaction on his face. It had been a long time since he'd been behind the wheel, but she understood men and their machines. He put it in gear and took off a little too fast. When he hit the brake, Lauren lurched forward. Instinctively Jake took his hand off the steering wheel to brace her and the car jerked. In a second it straightened as well-maintained, high-powered vehicles were designed to do. Still he quickly moved his hand back, fighting the wheel, stomping on the brake and causing more jerks.

"I mentioned it was a high-powered vehicle. Be kind to it." Lauren gestured at the steering wheel.

"I told you I couldn't drive," he said angrily.

She ignored the protest. "That was only your first time. Try it again."

He calmed down and asked, "Are you all right?"

"I'm fine." She put her hand on his arm and squeezed, but quickly released him. "Try it."

Jake looked over the steering wheel. He slowly released the brake and the car rolled forward. He stopped, then started again. Lauren realized he was testing the brake. Like a teenager at his first driving lesson, he went through the steps of getting to know the car. He took it slow until he felt comfortable.

"Great," Lauren praised. "You're doing fine."

She knew he didn't need her approval, but after her comment he spent the next twenty minutes driving back and forth through the parking lot, picking up speed and becoming more familiar with his skills. Several minutes later, he took the car out on the park's roads. They drove through the park, encountering no other cars. Jake was doing well. And he was smiling.

"Ready for the real road?" she asked.

He pulled into another parking lot and stopped the car. When he swung around to get out, she grabbed his arm. Muscles tensed under her hand.

"Don't get out," she said. "You're driving us back."

"No." He elongated the word. "I've already proved—"

"That you needed a little practice and you can do anything you set your mind to."

Jake only looked at her for a long moment.

Lauren nodded. "Yes, I believe that."

"Are you sure?" he asked.

"Absolutely."

"Your confidence is better than mine."

Lauren shifted in her seat. She faced him head-on. "You drive back and when we get close to the tunnel, I'll take over—deal?"

He didn't take a moment before agreeing.

"I'll at least give it a try, but if either of us thinks I'm a danger, we stop and you drive."

"Deal," she said. "But you'll do great."

JAKE DIDN'T STOP driving when they approached the Holland Tunnel. Neither did he relinquish control of the car when he started driving the streets from Chinatown to the Dakota. He pulled into the garage and cut the engine. Neither he nor Lauren moved.

"Enjoyed it, did you?" she asked.

He didn't hide his joy. "I did."

"See, I was right. You can do anything you put your mind to."

Jake knew she was thinking of their conversation about him consulting or writing or doing something that didn't require the use of his right arm. Jake couldn't help but agree with her. The car had shown him he could go where he wanted without a companion, without his brother being on hand. As a teenager, his first car had given him his freedom. He could go places his bicycle never took him. And oh, the places he went.

Lauren turned to get out. Jake's hand on her shoulder stopped her. "Thank you," he said.

His words meant a lot more than they seemed.

"You're welcome."

She tried to move again, but he pulled her back. Lauren stared at him. The air in the car was heavy and electric. He pulled her close and kissed her lightly on the mouth. Lauren didn't resist, but he could sense her confusion and regret.

Neither spoke until they were in the apartment.

"I'm going to go and clean up," she said, opening the door.

"You'll be down for dinner?"

She nodded.

Jake thought he'd lost all feeling in his body from his arm to his toes, but when he kissed Lauren he discovered that wasn't true. He admitted she was having an effect on him that he hadn't wanted, or at least hadn't thought he wanted. Now he knew he wanted more out of life than sitting around brooding about the past.

And he had her to credit for it. It was a miracle that he ran into her that day and that she goaded him into lunch. Where would he be today without that chance encounter?

Jake glanced at the door to her bedroom. What was she thinking in there? Had his kiss overstepped their boundaries? In the park, she said as much, but in the car she hadn't stopped him. He felt she wanted more.

Was it his arm that had her pushing back? Jake rejected that thought. She'd immediately made it apparent that she cared little about his arm other than to make sure he was in no pain. Where others shied away from even mentioning it, Lauren took on the subject without reserve. She touched him often and he liked her touch. He could feel the warmth of her hands and the miracle of her fingers as she massaged his shoulder and upper biceps. Lately, that touch had felt more than clinical.

Taking one more look at Lauren's door, Jake bounded up the steps and went to his own room. Twenty minutes later he was back, showered and dressed in fresh clothes. Lauren was in the kitchen.

"What are we having tonight?" he asked jovially, masking the strange way he really felt. That picnic today had thrown him. No, he told himself. That was a lie. It was the way Lauren had looked under the bright sunlight, the way he felt when she touched him and that sudden need to kiss her. He felt like that now. She opened the refrigerator and took out a container, yet all he could think of was the way her hair fell against her shoulders and how he wanted to brush it back.

"We're having a gourmet dish—spaghetti and meatballs." She laughed, holding up the bowl of spaghetti.

"Actually, it's a favorite of mine."

"Really?"

The question in her voice was defining. He realized how much she didn't know about him and how little he knew about her.

"Set the table," she said.

Jake moved to comply. This was his favorite part of the day. Usually, the housekeeper would prepare their meals and set the table, but when they were late, she left the food in the refrigerator and they only had to heat it up. They worked together well. Jake admitted he was going to miss Lauren when she left. She'd told him in the beginning that if she was hired it was temporary. She was going.

Jake tried to broach the subject this afternoon, but she pivoted any discussion back to him and he didn't challenge it. But now he wasn't looking forward to her leaving. He wouldn't have anyone else to step in. There was no one he would want to replace her.

"Do you cook your own spaghetti or was it your mother's that you preferred?"

He finished setting the table. "It was my housekeeper's. My mother didn't cook."

"You were a regular kid once?"

"Yes." Again he drew out the word. "Don't you think I could have been?"

They slipped into the chairs as they had done before, each taking the same place.

"At first I thought you were born full grown, holding your medical degree, but already experienced in every aspect of surgery."

"That's insulting," he said, but not with anger.

"I said *at first*."

"What do you think now?"

"That you're not as afraid as you once were," she said.

Jake couldn't help the small chuckle. She was very observant. He wasn't as afraid.

"I can credit you for that."

"Thank you." She smiled. "So have you decided on anything?"

"Consulting work. I'm doing it by video conference…at least at the beginning." He emphasized the last phrase, stopping her from speaking. Jake knew her argument would be that he should get out and inter-act with people in person. Maybe he would, but not yet. "What is your favorite food?"

"It isn't the food exactly. What I love about cooking is the company, people pre-paring it, the fun in discussing things while you work. The food always tastes best that way because of the love you put in it."

"Wow," he said. "What are we talking about?"

"Family," she answered. "They don't have to be blood related. Friends count too."

"So you can eat liverwurst?"

"I happen to like liverwurst. I also like bratwurst, bockwurst, knackwurst and weisswurst."

"So sausage is your thing?"

She laughed. "Yes."

"We'll have to add those to the menu."

"There's a diner near where I went to

school that served them all. We used to go there after class and eat tons of them."

Lauren looked so happy. He'd rarely seen her look otherwise. There was a sadness he'd noticed in her eyes a while ago, but lately it had disappeared. He wondered what had put it there and he hoped being around him had caused her to lose it. Even though he hadn't been the most welcoming in the beginning.

"Why don't we go to see a movie?" he said.

From Lauren's reaction, that was the last thing she expected to hear him say.

"You mean in a theater or in the room with the big-screen television?"

"I thought of going to a theater, but if you'd rather stay in and watch something here…" He left the sentence hanging.

"I would rather go out," she said. "But not tonight. It's been a long day. Maybe we could watch something here and go out Thursday."

Jake recognized her companion voice. It had been an experience for him and she didn't want to stretch the day's activities too far.

He nodded. "What would you like to see?"

"You know I'd pick a sappy romcom and you'd hate it, so why don't you make the decision. Just don't choose something too gory."

"I don't like gore."

"Too much like medicine?" she teased.

"I can't stand the sight of blood," he retorted, good-naturedly.

Lauren got up, taking her plate. "You go choose a movie. I'll clean these up and meet you."

Jake stood, but didn't immediately leave. Typically, they cleaned up together. He piled his silverware and glass on his plate and took it to the sink. Lauren accepted them with a smile. He stepped back several feet, before turning and going to find a DVD. Seconds later, Jake searched through his collection, rejecting almost everything. Too long, too much profanity, too little story.

"What did you choose?" she asked, coming into the room and curling up on the sofa.

"I have three I'm deciding on." He showed her the covers. "If you like Bruce Willis, we can watch any of the *Die Hard* action movies. If you're in the mood for the supernatural, I have a wide array of Stephen King adaptations. Or if you want to check out a black-and-white classic, there's Hitchcock's version of *The 39 Steps*."

She pointed to the last one.

"*The 39 Steps* it is."

He placed the DVD in the machine and joined her on the sofa.

"I thought of making popcorn, but we just ate dinner," Lauren said.

"Does white or red wine go with popcorn?" Jake lifted a bottle of wine from the table in front of them. Two glasses sat next to it. Lauren had no idea how long he'd practiced lifting both the wine and the glasses without dropping either. He also managed to pull the cork out and allow the wine to breathe. Now that the opening credits were running, he poured the two glasses and they settled back to watch.

"Have you seen this before?" Jake asked her.

"Many times. It's one of my favorites."

"Mine too," Jake said.

He lowered the lights and they silently concentrated on the movie. At least Lauren concentrated on it. He couldn't keep his mind on discovering the message of

The 39 Steps. He was more concerned with the woman next to him. Their day had been momentous and by all rights he should be exhausted, but instead he was exhilarated. She'd forced him to step outside his comfort zone, not with hostility or anger, but with cajoling and teasing. He liked it when she teased him.

Lauren unfolded her legs and stretched them out on the coffee table. Her foot kicked a magazine and it fell on the floor. She leaned forward and looked down.

"I'll get it later," she said almost to herself.

Repositioning herself, she was slightly closer to Jake than before. He wondered if she knew it or if she was just making herself more comfortable. For several more minutes he tried to follow the story.

When he glanced at Lauren, she'd fallen asleep, her breathing even. He reached over and removed the wineglass from her hand, setting it on the table. As he sat back, she slipped sideways and fell against him. Jake let her rest there, while he held his breath. Then he pushed her up and repositioned her on his shoulder as the movie played out. When the final scene came and went,

Jake let the DVD run to the end. Lauren still rested next to him and he was reluctant to move or he'd disturb her. Yet his arm was going numb from her lying against it.

He slipped away from her, and she shifted on the sofa, but didn't wake. Jake lowered her to the sofa. In the dim light of the room, she was beautiful. She no longer smelled of sunshine and grass as she had when they left the park. The floral scent of her soap and shampoo filled his nostrils and he forced himself not to wake her. Kneeling, he moved her legs from the table to the sofa.

Finding a blanket, he draped it over her and silenced the television. The room was thrown into semidarkness. Jake blinked a couple of times to let his eyes adjust.

He reached to collect the wineglasses and stepped on the magazine. The space between the table and the sofa forced him to drop down on his knees. As he reached down to pick it up, his face was close to Lauren's. He stopped in case she woke. She stirred, but settled without opening her eyes.

Quickly, Jake stood up and moved away. The urge to stay and watch her was strong. He went to his room and closed the door, but his thoughts remained in the room downstairs where the princess lay waiting for her prince to kiss her awake.

Jake had said he was no prince, but at the moment he seriously thought of making that fantasy a reality.

CHAPTER SEVEN

"Owww," Lauren screamed. She was falling and suddenly she stopped, hitting the bottom. Her heart thundered and fear that she'd killed herself knocked the breath out of her. Opening her eyes in the small space, she fought for freedom. Then memory came back. She was still in the television room. She'd fallen off the sofa. If she hadn't bumped her arm against the table, she'd laugh at herself.

Groaning, she pushed herself upright, looking for Jake. Where was he? The room was softly lighted, but she was alone. Her eyes fell on the digital numbers on the cable box. It was after three in the morning. There was a soft blanket that she was now sitting on. Jake must have put it over her. She stroked it, silently thanking him for his compassion.

Thirst woke her. Her throat was dry and

burning. She got up and wove around furniture and into the kitchen. The water was ice cold and delicious. She drank a full bottle and took a second one to go to her room. The view stopped her. The city wasn't asleep as New York never fully rested, but there was a calm to it. She could feel it in the way it looked back at her.

Lauren realized she would miss New York when she left. She sank down on the piano bench and thought about her time here. She'd come to New York straight out of Johns Hopkins medical school. She thought life would be perfect, but it had a way of disappointing you. Lauren knew her brushes with life were only scrimmages until Naliani died.

Tears flew to her eyes and she quickly brushed them away. Raising her head, she looked at the sky. It was dark and starless. She knew the stars were there, but the wash of city light, even at this hour, hid them from view. Could Naliani see them? Was she looking down on her mother and wondering why they were no longer together?

Her death was the reason Lauren had decided to start over. She'd move from this city and find a place where no one knew her, where no one could ask about her child and where there were no reminders of the times and places they had gone together. And then she'd seen Caleb's ad. Now she was here, postponing her plans and working with a man who had no idea who she was. And if he found out, she'd disappear from his life, this time forever.

"Lauren?"

She jumped at the sound of her name in the darkness. Even though it was spoken softly, the unexpectedness of it startled her.

"Why are you sitting in the dark?" Jake asked.

She swallowed, knowing she couldn't speak with the tears still stinging her eyes.

"Lights," she said, unable to utter more than one word. She was sure he couldn't see her and that helped her get herself under control before she had to speak again. "I woke up and the city looked so pretty."

She wondered why he was awake, but she didn't ask.

"You were sleeping so peacefully and the day had been long. I didn't want to wake you," he explained.

"I had a nice time today," she said.

Jake came down the stairs and walked to the piano.

"Do you play?" he asked.

She shook her head. "I had a few lessons when I was a child, but I didn't stick with it."

Jake took a seat next to her on the bench. He wore a robe over his pajamas.

"Will you—?"

He ran his fingers over several keys. Lauren recognized an arpeggio. She smiled at him even though her heart wasn't in it. She'd asked him about the piano before and he hadn't said he played it. The changes in him the last few weeks made her think he was returning to the man he was before the accident. She should encourage him to play. Yesterday she would have pushed him to try, but right now she had her own wounds to lick.

"Lauren, is something wrong?"

Jake didn't look at her. His fingers continued to skate over the keys. They were tentative at times as if he hadn't practiced in a long while. She knew that to be true, but his proficiency would return quickly once the use of his arm came back. She didn't know why she thought it would. He'd made so much progress in just the short time she'd been with him. He was on the road to recovery even if he didn't yet know it.

"There's nothing wrong," she said.

"You're awfully quiet. For someone who loves to talk, your silence feels like shouting."

"I'm sorry." Lauren looked away from Jake. "I guess sleeping on the sofa made me a little groggy." She couldn't tell him the real reason for her mood. It's not that he wouldn't understand, but she couldn't relate the story without dissolving into tears. The pain of loss was too close to the surface.

His one-handed piano playing continued. And then it struck a raw nerve. Lauren almost hopped off the bench when the happy notes of "Twinkle, Twinkle Little Star" filled the cavernous room. The water bottle she'd been holding fell to the floor.

"I think I'll go to bed now," she said. Leaving the water, she held herself erect and walked as normally as she could up the stairs and into her room. She didn't undress, just lay on the bed and crawled into a fetal position. Tomorrow would be better, she told herself. Tomorrow she'd move Naliani back into the safe place in her heart where she lived and resume her duties to Jake.

Lauren closed her eyes wondering if sleep would elude her, but she fell asleep within minutes. When she woke, the sun was blaring through the windows. The bedside clock said it was after ten. She sat up straight, restricted by the shirt and pants she'd changed into after she and Jake returned from their picnic. Quickly, she went through her morning routine and headed downstairs. The apartment was quiet. As she looked over the railing, she didn't see Jake, but reaching the bottom of the steps, she heard him speaking in his office. She smiled. Since she'd arrived, she'd never seen him in that room. She heard his muffled voice. He was on the phone. Hopefully, he'd begun his consulting.

In the kitchen, the housekeeper was still there and coffee was ready.

"How about some breakfast?" she asked with no censure for the late hour in her voice. Lauren was used to being up early. In her previous life, she was usually in her office at 7:00 a.m. Her first patient was scheduled at nine. Sleeping until after ten was unlike her.

"I'd love some." She took a drink of her coffee. "Have you seen Dr. Masters this morning?"

"He was in that room when I arrived and he hasn't come out. The coffee was made and there were fresh bagels on the counter. I think he took his own breakfast."

"Thanks," Lauren said. "He must be ready for something else by now."

"I'll make him a tray," the housekeeper said.

"I'll take it when it's ready. I think he's speaking to someone from the hospital."

"Good," she said with a smile.

Lauren was finishing her second cup of coffee and the last of her toast when the tray was ready. She knocked softly on the door and opened it. Jake was on the phone, but waved her in. She heard the familiar medical jargon and smiled inwardly. After setting the tray near the desk, she picked up his coffee cup and an empty plate that held crumbs and a smear of cream cheese and returned to the kitchen.

The housekeeper took the dishes and Lauren found herself with nothing to do. Jake sounded as if he'd be a while on the phone.

Her thoughts from the night before came back to her. It had been a long while since she allowed memories of Naliani to break through her resolve. But today she would confront them.

JAKE CAUGHT UP WITH Lauren after his phone call. He swung her around in a mock dance.

"My, you're in a mood today," she said.

"Let's go for a drive," he suggested.

"A drive where?"

"Does it matter? Let's just get in the car and follow where it leads us."

"Okay," Lauren said. Her mood lightened. "I'll get my purse."

She also got a blazer and changed into pressed jeans and slipped on a pair of high-heeled shoes. To be safe, she added casual shoes to a shoe bag. Wherever they were going, she could be either casual without the jacket or neatly dressed with it. They drove to Connecticut, taking the Merritt Parkway. Jake commented on the art deco bridges as they passed under them.

"Who knew you were such a font of non-medical information?" she said when he'd parked the car and they were sitting at an outdoor ice cream stand eating identical boats of banana splits.

"You'd be surprised," he said. "Just as I would. What are your nonkindergarten talents?"

"Brain surgery," she teased.

Jake shook his head.

"Tap dancer?"

He glanced at her legs. "A possibility," he said. "You've got the legs for it."

"Keep your eyes on your ice cream," she said.

Jake shrugged. "Seriously, what do you do other than take care of kids?"

"I make pop-up books."

"What?" His voice was a mixture of laughter and wonder. "That's something you do with your kids in class."

"Not these. They're very elaborate and not for kindergartners."

"Really, so they're not trees or a house that comes up when you turn the page?"

"Yes and no," she answered. "The concept is the same, but the elaborate house that pops up could match this elaborate apartment you live in."

"Wow, I need to see these. How did you get into that?"

"At first I did it for relaxation. I made one in a craft class and it took forever, but after I got the mechanics down, I loved the result. So I kept at it. I have some very complicated designs."

"Where are they?"

"Right now they're in storage until I decide where I'm settling."

"So you haven't made a decision on that yet?"

She shook her head.

"I'm getting closer."

They finished their banana splits and went back to his car.

DRIVING DOWN THE HIGHWAY, Jake's heart thumped. He realized he didn't want her to go. He'd become used to her being there. He even enjoyed their arguments. Sometimes he looked forward to them. But she had to be thinking of returning to work. And why wouldn't she? He'd taken her suggestions and he was all the better for them.

"Lauren, I like having you here. If you

can postpone leaving until Cal returns, I'd appreciate that."

Jake wanted to look at Lauren as he spoke, but he was driving and could only glance at her. She appeared at a loss for words. He didn't think she'd expected him to say that. He hadn't intended to, but he liked talking to her. He liked her more than as a friend, but he couldn't go further than that. He remembered her first day, when she walked into the apartment and had to pry him out of bed. Now he was asking her not to leave.

"I…" she began. "I have to…"

"Don't answer now," he told her. She was faltering and he didn't want her to refuse before she had time to process the request. "Give yourself time to think about it."

She nodded. Jake saw her head bob up and down. He wondered if he'd shocked her with his admission.

It had certainly shocked him.

He pulled the car off the parkway and headed toward a place where they could talk. Eventually, he found an abandoned office park. The buildings were in various stages of demolition. The parking lot was cracked and weeds were seeping up through the breakage. He pulled up and cut the engine.

He came around and helped her out.

"What are we doing here?" she asked, looking around.

"Nothing in particular. Just giving us a rest."

"Good." She smiled. "Because I have a surprise for you."

Jake could see she was back to being the playful yet strong woman he'd found her to be that day he'd run into her on the street.

"What's the surprise?"

"Wait over there for a moment. I have to get it." He did as she asked. Moments later she took his arm and led him back to the car.

"What is that?" Jake asked when he got in and saw the gadget attached to the steering wheel.

"It's called a steering wheel knob. It allows you to use less effort to turn the car."

"You think I need a crutch?" he asked, affronted.

"It's a safety feature, Jake. Isn't part of the Hippocratic Oath to do no harm?"

He turned in the seat and stared at her.

"You know you should have been a lawyer. You're wasted as a kindergarten teacher."

"I'll take that as a compliment," Lauren said.

Jake laughed. "You would."

"It'll make steering easier for you."

He frowned at her.

"Don't knock it until you've tried it."

"So what's the point?" he asked.

"Safety first," she said. "It concentrates the force in one place and makes turning a lot simpler. Try it."

"It'll ruin the steering wheel."

"There's a rubber cushion against the wheel so it will not cause any abrasions. Now stop putting up obstacles and see how it works."

"Where did you find this thing?"

"I used one when I first learned to drive."

"Now we learn the truth."

"It helped," she said. "My father installed it on the family car and I felt like I knew what I was doing. I'd sit at a light and when it turned green, I'd spin that knob and the car would turn on a dime."

"Is this your father's?" Jake asked.

She shook her head. "His was a plain silver knob. They come in colors now." She pointed to the one on the steering wheel. "I saw some that looked like the wheel of a car with a hub cap in a choice of colors, but I thought you'd like this one with the medical insignia on it."

"I don't need a knob."

"You don't need to drive either, but you like it. So I'm trying to keep the other cars on the road safe from you. Now drive."

He smiled. Jake liked getting her upset. So far she hadn't caught on to his antics, but she was a smart woman and eventually she would. He put the car in gear and, using the knob, turned circles around the empty parking lot.

"Wow," he said. "I like this."

He drove faster and turned corners harder.

"Don't do it too fast," she said.

"I won't do it on the road," he said, taking another fast turn. "Why didn't you tell me how much fun this was?"

Lauren sat still and said nothing. Jake made several turns around the lot and then slowed down. He drove up and down to show Lauren he wasn't going to hurt anyone when he was back on the road. She was right about the small knob on the steering wheel. It handled a lot of the force needed to turn the wheel, making it easier for him to use with only one hand.

After he'd driven several miles in the lot, he stopped the car and turned the engine off.

"Thank you, Lauren."

"You're welcome," she said.

Jake saw the small smile that curved the corners of her lips. She did that often when she didn't want him to know how pleased she was with something he'd accomplished or accepted.

He drove back toward the city. Changing lanes was monumentally easier with the knob than without it. He was amazed at how attuned she was to his needs. He was used to being on the other side, attending to his patients. He never thought he needed anyone to take care of him. But Lauren had shown him that everyone needs someone.

And she wasn't bad to have around. In fact, he wanted her to stay. She had to say she would stay.

For the first time, he wasn't looking forward to Cal's return.

CHAPTER EIGHT

IGNORING A QUESTION wasn't something Lauren usually did, especially as a doctor. Though Jake's question wasn't medical, it required an answer. And it had to be that she couldn't stay. He was on the road to recovery and she didn't think he'd relapse if she wasn't part of his daily routine.

He'd helped her too, Lauren thought. Having someone else to focus on had kept her from thinking about her own problems. She still planned to leave and start over somewhere else, and she couldn't wait for Caleb to return. She needed a finite date. She was becoming too attached to Jake. And right now she had too much on her mind to begin a relationship.

She was making a giant assumption in thinking she could have a relationship with Jake. He probably wasn't open to that, despite his statement that he liked having her around. He could say the same of a maid, but she knew that wasn't the case.

A week later Jake had not asked his question again and Lauren had not brought up the subject. But she had thought about it. Few other things occupied her mind. Each day Jake took Lauren for a drive. At first, Lauren would drive one way and Jake the other. She could hardly remember when things changed and he was driving both ways.

"I've been thinking about that movie we were supposed to go to," Jake said while he drove out of the city one Saturday afternoon.

"What were you thinking?"

"Why don't we go tonight? We could get something to eat and then drive to a movie."

Lauren thought about it. "You do know what tonight is," she said.

He frowned. "Saturday?"

"That's right."

"What's wrong with Saturday?"

"It's date night. There will be lots of couples going to movies. Shouldn't we wait for a weeknight?" she said. She didn't mention that young lovers liked to hold on to each other in dark theaters.

"That's all right," he said. "I mean, we know this is not a date. If you don't want to go, we can—"

"That's not it," Lauren interrupted. "I only wanted to remind you that you're likely to find more going on in the theater than on the screen."

"I think I can handle that. Now what shall we see?"

Jake had chosen the movie they watched in the apartment. So over a light dinner in a Jersey diner, Lauren checked her phone and found several current movies that were playing. She tried to avoid the most popular movies but in the end Jake said he'd really like to see the recently released action adventure that was advertised on television and billboards all over the city.

The line for the movie wrapped around the building. Lauren held on to Jake's right arm. People talked around them, their voices blending into white noise. Inside the apartment, Jake sometimes wore a sling. It was an indicator to Lauren that he was in pain. When they went out he'd take it with them but rarely put it on. With her holding his arm, no one knew he couldn't move it.

"It looks like this is a good choice," Jake said.

"The marketing machine for this movie has been ramped up and spewing out teasers for a month. You see it advertised everywhere."

Jake shrugged as if he hadn't noticed until today. He watched some television, but lately he'd been spending a lot of time on the video hookup he had with the hospital. She secretly thought he was also writing.

"You'll love it," Lauren said. "It has—"

"Lori!" Someone called her name.

She looked around. Because she was holding on to Jake, her movement pulled him with her.

"Lori, that is you."

Coming toward her was the last person she wanted to see. He could blow everything if she didn't control the conversation. They hadn't seen each other in a year and Lauren was surprised when he grabbed her and pulled her into a bear hug. Her arm was nearly wrenched from Jake's and she felt him flinch as if in pain.

"Hello, Richard," she said.

He was with a beautiful woman, who curled her arm around his.

"What are you doing here? I thought you moved to LA."

"I did. I'm just visiting." The woman at his side pulled on his arm and he glanced at her and then back at Lauren. "Oh, Lori, this is Amber West."

Her voice was as strong as her grip on Richard's arm. "Nice to meet you," she said.

Lauren turned to Jake. "Jake, this is Richard Peterson, my ex-husband."

She kept her eyes on Jake. He didn't react, but put his left hand over hers. Lauren knew it wasn't a message he was sending to her ex-husband, but a way of preventing him from shaking hands.

"So, I guess we're all here to see the movie," Amber said. Her voice was slightly high. She had drop-dead-gorgeous model looks and her makeup was flawless. Lauren didn't judge her or Richard. Their separation and divorce had been amicable. Naliani was the catalyst that had forced them to confront the truth. They were no longer in love and parting was beneficial to them both. While Lauren mourned their lost child, she never mourned her marriage.

The line began to move and Lauren sighed

with relief. She said it was nice to see Richard again and acknowledged Amber. Jake kept her arm in his as they went into the darkened theater. Lauren saw her ex-husband and his new girlfriend and moved as far from them as she could get.

"Are these all right?" she asked Jake, indicating seats near the rear of the theater.

"Are you all right?" he asked. "We can leave if you want."

She shook her head and sat down in the reclining chair that theatergoers expected these days. Pushing back, she raised the concealed footrest.

"How about some popcorn?"

Lauren moved to get up, but Jake stopped her. "I'll get it," he said.

She didn't argue with him. He needed to be independent. This was his way of showing her he could do for himself. It was also his way of letting her know that he was conquering the world by no longer trying to hide his arm.

He left and when he returned, the sling was over his right arm. Nestled inside it were two soft drinks. His left hand held a king-size tub of popcorn. Lauren took the tub and then one of the drinks. Jake sat down with the other. She noticed a smug look on his face. It was a baby step, but he'd taken it and conquered it. She wanted to congratulate him, but knew he would tell her that he wasn't trying to prove anything. She gave him a smile, silently communicating her thoughts. She realized he couldn't know what she was thinking, but she felt he understood that she was pleased for him.

The lights dimmed and the movie began. They sat back and watched. The story was about an ordinary man and wife on the brink of divorce who make a wrong turn and get caught up in plans for a deadly terrorist attack. The chase begins and from then on it's nonstop action as they get separated and try to find each other, depending on each other to stay alive, and stay a step away from the terrorists trying to kill them. At one point, Lauren noticed Jake tense. On the screen an explosion took place. Several people were lying on the ground bleeding. She put her hand on his and a second later realized he'd curled one finger of his right hand over hers. She stared at his hand, forgetting the action on the screen. Jake didn't seem to notice. By the end of the two hours, the main characters were back in love and glad to be alive.

If only it was that easy, Lauren thought. Relationships were complicated. She glanced in the direction where Richard and Amber had been seated but they were gone. She'd once been in love with Richard, planned to spend her life with him, but things changed.

Jake got up. Both drink cups were empty. The tub held the dregs of popcorn kernels, some unpopped. They placed the cups inside and joined the exiting crowds.

"What did you think?" he asked when they were on the street.

Lauren wanted to bring up the movement of his hand, but she decided this wasn't the time. If he was aware of it, he'd say something.

"I liked it," she told him. "Some of the action sequences were improbable, but I like action movies, so I always forgive Hollywood for doing the impossible. What did you think?"

"I think that the trauma of surviving terrorists will not make a couple fall in love."

He focused on the love plot. That wasn't

something she would have expected, but Jake was always doing the unexpected.

"They were already in love. They just didn't know it," she said.

"You don't really believe that, do you?"

"Of course I do. Just because a couple has problems doesn't mean they don't love each other."

"What about you and Richard. Did you have problems and were still in love?"

Lauren closed her eyes for a second. She'd walked right into that one. "We did," she said carefully. "But there came a time when we were no longer in love and living together didn't make sense. As you can see, we parted as friends."

"It looked like you two are more than friends."

Lauren had been surprised when Richard hugged her. They'd often greet each other that way when they were married, but they were no longer the same people. She was with Jake. The fact that Richard didn't know she wasn't dating Jake was beside the point. He had a date. Hugging an ex-wife or even an ex-girlfriend when you were with someone else seemed inappropriate.

"I guess we are more than friends," she said. "We were married. I was once in love with him."

Jake stopped and turned to her. "And you're not now?"

She shook her head. "No, now we're just friends."

"More than friends," he corrected her.

He was acting like a jealous lover. They'd shared one kiss and one almost kiss. They had no relationship, so he couldn't be jealous.

"You and I are also more than friends."

"We are?" His eyebrows rose. "How's that?"

"We've kissed."

IT WASN'T LIKELY that Jake would forget kissing Lauren. Given the fact that he wanted to kiss her again. All the feelings he thought dead came back to life when she was around. The kiss had been in the back of his mind for weeks. And that night, he'd tested the waters. They'd proved addictive, but so far he'd had enough self-control to resist.

He'd almost caved sitting in the darkened theater, especially after meeting her ex-husband.

She had an ex-husband.

He appeared to have moved on, if Jake read the woman on his arm correctly. Yet Lauren was taking longer in her recovery. Jake had seen it in her eyes when she first spoke of her past. Lately, he believed the darkness in her had lifted somewhat. Each of them had their own demons. She'd forced his out of him, though she told him she'd never been a companion before. Jake had had nurses and personal assistants. Lauren acted more like a nurse, aware of changes in him. In the theater, she took his hand when the explosion happened. Jake knew it was coming. The charges had been set. They had to go off sometime. Lauren was right there, silently helping him through anything that he might be affected by.

He wanted her to stay, but he couldn't force that outcome. They hadn't talked about it since he suggested it. There was a lot he wanted to discuss.

"Tired?" he asked when they were back in the apartment.

"Not much," she said.

"Good. Let's talk."

Jake led her to the sofa in the room with the huge windows overlooking the city. She slipped her feet out of her shoes and made herself comfortable.

"What do you want to chat about?"

"Ex-husbands."

He watched Lauren carefully, noticing her go still for a few seconds.

"I have an ex-husband."

"You don't have to tell me about him. It's not my business, but I didn't know you'd been married."

She didn't have to say that there was a world of things he didn't know about her. Jake knew there was.

"Richard is an architect. We were married for several years," she said.

Nonspecific, Jake thought, but let it go.

"We grew apart. After the divorce, he moved to Los Angeles."

"I'm sure there's more to it than that."

Lauren got up and walked about the room. She paused in front of the massive windows, then moved past the piano before turning to face Jake. She wore a short-sleeved blouse and long pants that had his eyes focusing on her legs. It took her a while to begin to speak. Jake waited.

"We met at a party. He gave me his number and I called him."

Jake believed that. He thought of how she'd nearly accosted him on the street and here she'd ended up standing across the room from him in his own apartment.

"We dated for nearly a year before he asked me to marry him. I was in love or thought I was. And so we were married."

"Then what?"

Lauren didn't speak for a long time. Finally she looked around and moved to pick up her purse before taking the chair across from him. Leaning forward, she put her elbows on her knees and lowered her face to her hands. Jake didn't know if she was about to cry or what. They hadn't turned on bright lights, but neither was the room dark.

"Lauren, are you all right?"

Jake thought she might be thinking of her ex-husband. Despite what she said about not being in love with him, was this sadness due to her ex and the fact that tonight he'd returned to her memory if not her life?

She looked up and opened the purse. It took a second for her to find what she was searching for. She pulled a small piece of paper out and passed it to him. Jake turned the lamp on next to him and looked at the paper. It was a photo of a little girl. Jake wasn't good at estimating the age of children, especially from a photo, but he'd say the dark-eyed child was about four or five. She smiled up from the paper. Jake smiled back at her.

"She's beautiful. Who is she?"

"My daughter."

She spoke so quietly, Jake wasn't sure he'd heard her. "You have a daughter?" he confirmed.

"Had."

Her voice cracked. Jake came forward in his chair, shifting to the edge of the sofa. Lauren reached for the photo. He handed it back and she returned it to her purse.

"She died three years ago."

"How? From what?" His medical training went on alert.

"Bacterial meningitis," she said. "One day she was fine and that night, I was rushing her to the ER. Twenty-four hours later, I was no longer a mother."

Jake moved. He couldn't stop himself. He was next to her in a second, putting his arm around her. "I am so sorry. I didn't know."

"Of course you didn't."

"This is why you're leaving the city?" he asked.

She nodded quickly. "After Naliani died, Richard and I had nothing to connect us. We'd grown apart, wanted different things in life. Mostly, I wanted to shut myself off from everyone and everything. If it hadn't been for my friend, I'd probably still be hiding in bed, refusing to go anywhere or see anyone."

Jake knew exactly what she meant. That's how he'd been when she came into his life. He didn't know at the time that she understood his experience. She knew what he was doing because she had been there. She understood the destructiveness of his actions and she wasn't going to let him continue.

"Naliani, that was her name?"

Lauren smiled quickly as if a thought about the child had come to mind. "We called her LeeLee. When she was learning to talk, she couldn't say her name."

Jake squeezed her shoulder and pushed himself back onto the sofa. He still sat on the edge, in case he needed to go to her quickly.

"Speaking of that, Jake, I can't stay here much longer. I have to make decisions on what I'm going to do and where I plan to do it."

Jake didn't want to have this conversation now. Her emotions were too close to the surface.

"You're a really intelligent woman. And you know that today is not the time to think of making a major change."

"We both know this decision isn't being made at this moment. The day I met you, I told you I was planning to leave. Seeing my ex-husband tonight and telling you about Naliani don't play into the decision."

"Wait a minute," Jake said. "Your mother and your child died within two years of each other." It wasn't a question, but an observation.

Lauren didn't say anything.

"That has to play into the sense of urgency you suddenly feel."

She dropped her head, an indication that he'd found his mark.

"Promise me you'll stay until Cal returns."

"I can't agree to that. I don't know when he's due to come back," she said.

Neither did Jake. For a change, she was the vulnerable one and he wanted to keep her safe.

"You said we were more than friends. This friend wants to be your companion."

"Role reversal," Lauren said and began to laugh.

Immediately, Jake recognized that it wasn't a mirthful laugh. She was not going to be able to stay in control of her emotions. She probably hadn't fully dealt with the loss of her child or the dissolution of her marriage and tonight both had confronted her without warning.

He reached for her, pulling her out of the chair and into his arms. "Breathe," he whispered. She trembled against him, struggling to get control of herself. "Breathe," he repeated and kept repeating it until she finally calmed.

Jake didn't let her go. He cradled her closer to him.

ONCE A DOCTOR... Lauren thought. She couldn't help keeping records. It was part and parcel of being in medicine. You needed to document every detail of a patient's care. Even though Jake didn't fit the strict guidelines for a patient, in her mind, he was one.

Lauren had a few minutes before meeting Amy, so she used them to update her file on Jake. It wasn't very long, but she noted the changes she'd seen in him, both psychological and physical. She was entering his progress on her computer when the screen announced she had a video message.

Clicking over to it, she saw it was from Jake's brother, Caleb.

"Hello," she said cheerfully.

"How are you?" he asked.

"Doing well," Lauren said. She knew he was getting the preliminaries out of the way. He was really interested in how Jake was doing. Caleb was as good-looking as his brother, although there were marked differences in their appearances. Caleb was rugged looking, sun drenched, hair lightened by working outside. She could easily see him on horseback galloping into the sunset after saving the day.

Jake was more serious, more private or self-possessed, keeping everything inside instead of allowing the world to determine who he was and what he was about. Lauren didn't know if he was different when he could do sports, taking risks for the thrill of it, but she thought he'd still have a persona that he allowed the world to see, but not the inner man.

Somehow she wanted to know that inner man.

"How's Jake adjusting?"

Finally, she had something good to report. "I think he's coming along. I coaxed him out of the apartment. We've been walking in the park. And recently we went for a long drive into New Jersey."

Caleb smiled. His face transformed. She thought it was a family trait. Jake's did the same, although his smiles were a rarity.

"How'd you do that?"

"I gave him no choice." She paused a moment. "Secretly, I think he wanted to get out, but his routine was set and he didn't see a reason to change it. But I'm a change in itself, in his routine, that is, so he didn't fight with me for long."

"Great. I am so glad to hear it."

Lauren left out that she let him drive. She didn't know how Caleb would react to that. Maybe he would think she was being reckless. After all, she'd been in this job for less than three months.

"Have you talked to him?" she asked.

"Not this week. He's still a little curt with me."

"He doesn't mean that," she jumped in.

"I know."

Caleb put a hand up as if the two of them were in the same room and he was trying to stop her from saying something.

"Jake has been down on himself so long, I don't think he knows he's doing it," Caleb said.

You didn't have to be a doctor to figure that out, Lauren thought.

"Maybe he'll be talking to me by his birthday," Caleb said.

"When is that?" Lauren asked.

"Next month. We used to always spend our birthdays together. Mine is a month later, so we'd get together on the halfway point."

"I think he's getting better. If he hasn't

come around by then, hopefully he'll be a lot different when you get back." Lauren held out hope. She understood that Caleb was concerned about Jake and his progress.

"If that happens, I'll call you a miracle worker," he said.

Caleb rang off then with his words still in her mind. She wasn't a miracle worker. She was only coaching someone into doing things he wanted to do and helping him to see the opportunities that lay before him.

Lauren knew she wasn't supposed to get attached to her patients. Since most of hers were children, she offered hugs as therapy. She wondered if that would work on Jake.

LAUREN COULDN'T START with hugs, but *love* might work. At least the *love* that was shouted over a ball and net.

"Those shoes won't do," Lauren said. "You need sneakers. Those are mainly deck shoes masquerading as sneakers. I'll get them."

She ran up the stairs and came back with a pair of black tennis shoes. Lauren didn't give him a chance to protest. She grabbed the slip-on shoes he wore and pulled them off, then quickly started to push his feet into the black sneakers.

"You're going to have to help me here," Lauren said. She couldn't get his feet in the shoes.

Jake didn't like needing help, she knew, but he complied. She tied the shoes and stood up. "Time to go," she said, cheerfully. She didn't want to look at his face. She expected it would be dark with rage. That didn't matter, but by the time the day was over, she expected he'd be really angry with her.

"Where are we going?" he asked as she sped along the highway. "And at this hour."

"Someplace you're familiar with." It was midnight on a Thursday, the slowest night of the week. Lauren pulled into a driveway.

"Oh no," he said. "What are we doing here?"

"We're going to play. I have a reservation."

"Who are you planning to play with?"

She parked the car and got out. Coming around to where Jake sat, she opened the door.

"Come on, we don't want to be late."

"I'm not going in there. What am I going to do at a tennis court, watch you play?"

"You're going to play," she said.

"I am not."

"Must you always fight every suggestion I have?" Lauren asked. "We're doing this, so get out of the car."

Jake slid out and they headed for the door. Lauren carried their equipment.

"I cannot play tennis, remember? I only have one arm."

"So you'll play with one arm."

"How? I have a two-handed backhand."

"Correction," she said. "You had a two-handed backhand. Now you have a one-handed one."

"Who wants to see someone playing with one hand?"

"You don't need to worry about that," she told him. "We have the place to ourselves. There are no other players. So, no need to feel self-conscious or to think people are staring at you."

"Lauren, I'm right-handed."

"Learn, Jake."

They were on the court. The lights were bright and Lauren set her bag down and pulled out two racquets. One was Jake's. She handed it to him. He hesitated, but took it finally.

He looked confused. "It's been restrung."

"Why are you surprised? You haven't used it in a while. It needed strings."

"Do I take it you can play?"

"Until I took yours to have it strung, I'd never had one in my hand. This means we're even. I've never played and you have to use your left hand."

She popped the cap on two cans of balls, dropped three of them at his feet and walked to the other side of the court.

"Ready?" she asked.

Jake stood there. He hadn't moved since she left his side.

"Too scared to try?" she asked.

"Calling me a chicken will not work," he shouted.

"How about a has-been, someone who's not willing to try again?"

She threw a ball in the air and hit it with her racquet. It crashed into the net.

"It's not a baseball," Jake stated.

"Then teach me what to do." She tried the same thing, tossing the ball up and hitting it with the racquet. The result was different. It sailed over the net like a fly ball and hit the heavy curtain at the back of the court.

Jake shook his head. He reached down, took the balls and stuffed them in his pockets. With the racquet in hand, he moved to the middle of the court.

"See how I'm standing?" he called.

Lauren nodded.

"You have to stand this way. Bounce the ball. Let's not start with tossing it. Then step in and hit it."

He demonstrated awkwardly. He had to both bounce the ball and then hit it with the racquet. As a right-handed person, the action was unusual, but the ball went over the net and practically landed at Lauren's feet.

"How am I supposed to hit a ball back when you put it right there? I can't move fast enough."

"That's the point of the game," Jake said. "Hit the ball where your opponent can't reach it."

He came to her side of the net and began teaching her what to do, how to hold the racquet, how to stand, where her feet should be, where she should strike the ball. Before she knew it, an hour had gone by. They got drinks of water.

"Are you tired?" Lauren asked.

Jake shook his head. "What about you?"

"I could go on, but I think this is enough for the day. We can come back tomorrow."

She smiled when she said that. She'd been right in thinking that he missed his sports and there was no reason he couldn't return to some of them. He wouldn't be any top-ranked player, that was for sure, but still. Lauren didn't know if he had been in the past. He'd enjoyed playing tennis and that was the goal she had in mind, that he enjoy the things he'd done and no longer thought he was able to do.

She knew there were activities that would be totally off the table, but there were many that he was still capable of participating in.

"Thank you, Lauren," Jake said as they entered the apartment. "You proved that you were right again. I enjoyed playing tonight. Even though it felt strange to use my left hand and I had to adjust my backhand and forehands to the opposite sides, it felt good to be back on the court."

Lauren's smile was ear to ear.

"Then we can go again without argument."

"Do I really argue against everything you suggest?"

"Saying good-morning might be an exception."

CHAPTER NINE

AMY REYNOLDS WAS an on-time person. When she ran Lauren's office, she was always in early and stayed late. She had a ready smile for a crying child and a sympathetic shoulder for a frantic parent. While sewing was a hobby she loved, nursing was her life. The two were going shopping and having an early dinner.

Jake was closeted in his office when she left. She told the housekeeper where she was going in case she was needed. It was her day off.

"You told him?" Amy said as they waded through reams of fabrics standing like spiral lollipops. They'd detoured into a tiny fabric shop.

"Almost everything."

"What did you hold back?" Amy asked.

"I didn't mention that I was a doctor," she said. She also didn't mention how she felt about Jake. She'd told him they were more than friends, but the fact that she wanted even more than that was her secret alone.

Amy pulled down a bolt of shimmering gold lamé.

"What are you going to make with that?" The fabric was beautiful and fell over Lauren's hand like a gold waterfall.

"Well, a nanny and princess have been done, but we can do a seventies disco dancer or a beauty queen with a fancy sash. What do you think?"

"No, thank you. I'm done with costumes and characters." That is except for the persona she was portraying.

"When are you going to tell him the whole truth?" Amy asked. She wasn't a fan of Lauren's deception. Lauren justified it by the small changes she saw in him. He had much less stress now than when she first met him. He was working with the hospital. And the night at the movie, when she touched his right hand, his finger curled.

"I don't know. He's asked me to stay on until his brother returns."

"When is that?"

"I don't know."

Amy stopped in the act of pulling down another bolt of fabric. Looking over her shoulder, she had a perplexing expression on her face.

"He asked you to stay open-ended?"

"Amy, I'm not an airline ticket."

"That's what it sounds like. Return at some future date to be determined."

While that sounded a little better, it was still like not having a date when the job was finished. Lauren reminded herself that it was a temporary job and by rights she should be gone already.

"He is making progress," Lauren said. "We went to the movies last night and during the film I saw his finger move."

"Wow," Amy said. "That is a really good sign."

Lauren knew her friend had switched from seamstress to nurse.

"What did he think?"

She put her hands on her hips and scanned the shelves. "I don't think he's aware of it."

"You didn't tell him?"

"The timing didn't seem right. We started talking about Richard, who we also bumped into at the movies. He has a new girlfriend."

"Looks like you, doesn't she?"

Lauren thought for a moment. The two of them were the same height, same hair color, same complexion. It came as a surprise that the woman with Richard, Amber, did look like her.

"Men can be like that. They go for the same type of woman all the time."

"Women aren't like that?" Lauren asked.

"Basically, they want the same type of personality, but the looks don't usually mimic their previous partner. Think about Jake. How does he compare to Richard?"

"They're polar opposites. Richard is kind and sensitive. Jake is gruff and wants his way all the time." As soon as the words left her mouth, Lauren wanted to take them back. She tried to cover herself. "Just to be clear," she said to Amy, "I had a relationship with Richard, but I am not in one with Jake. I'm his friend and his companion, nothing more."

"Really?" Amy's brows rose.

"Really," Lauren insisted.

"Then why does your voice soften when you talk about him?"

"It doesn't."

Amy went on as if Lauren hadn't said anything. "Why didn't you tell him about his hand? Or give him a definite date when you were leaving. You haven't even thought of a place to go yet. And why did you accept an open-ended ticket to ride?"

LAUREN WAS STILL thinking about Amy's question when she let herself into the apartment. It was after nine o'clock. They'd spent more time than expected at dinner, yet in the back of her mind Amy's question worried her.

Had she really left Jake with the impression that she was staying? She supposed she had. Lauren hadn't agreed to stay on, but she hadn't disagreed either. And she had no plans about where to go. When she put her personal items in storage, she'd planned to leave the city and travel a while, find a place to settle that felt right. She would talk to the local medical community and find out if the fit was right.

But none of that had happened. She saw the ad that Caleb placed and decided on the spur of the moment to satisfy her curiosity and see if Jake was the way she remembered from their college days.

"Lauren, where have you been?" Jake rushed down the steps. "I've been calling you all afternoon."

"What's wrong?" Lauren's heart kicked up a notch.

"You went missing."

"Jake, today is my day off. I wasn't missing and I left word with the housekeeper. Didn't she tell you?"

"She was gone by the time I came out of the office."

Lauren let out a breath, relieved that nothing had happened while she was away.

"I know I've told you in the past when I was going out, but you were busy with the hospital and I didn't want to interrupt."

His shoulders dropped. "I forgot. You're always here."

"I'm glad nothing happened. Did you eat?"

He nodded. "Where were you?"

"Out with a friend. We went shopping, then had dinner."

"All day?" His voice held a challenge.

Lauren lifted the bags in her hands. "Yes,

all day," she replied sarcastically. She'd bought a few personal items and a new dress. "I'm allowed," she emphasized.

After dropping the bags on a chair, she faced him and in a normal voice, asked, "What did you do today?"

"I consulted a lot. We were on the phone for hours."

"Why don't you go into the hospital and consult in person?"

He hadn't wanted to in the past, but Lauren thought he was ready to appear in public and not be self-conscious of his arm. There was also the movement of his finger. Amy had said she should talk to him about it. Maybe the function was returning.

"Are you tired?" she asked.

"Not especially," he said. "Why, are you?"

"I want to talk to you about something."

She hoped the discussion wouldn't have him trying to force his hand to move. It would add another level of stress to his life. Only recently had he seemed more relaxed.

Lauren gestured toward the sofa. The two of them sat down. Lauren purposely took a seat on his right.

"What do you want to talk about?"

She heard the caution in his voice. He was obviously expecting bad news.

"We went to the movies last night," she said.

He nodded.

"Did anything unusual happen while we were there?"

His eyebrows knitted, and he looked confused by her question. "Other than the two of us sitting in recliners, there wasn't much that was different than when we watched a movie here, except the place was filled with strangers, apart from your ex." He showed a small smile, one of those quick ones that were more anticipation of something to come than changing the mood.

Lauren looked down for a moment. Then she took Jake's hand and held it. He watched her closely. She knew he didn't understand what she was doing.

"Something unusual did happen in the theater." She was staring at his hand.

Jake did the same. "What?" he asked.

"Move your finger," she said.

"What?"

Lauren looked up. "In the theater, when the explosion came, you tensed."

He didn't nod or acknowledge the fact in any way.

"I took your hand." She paused, hoping he'd remember. She looked directly at him. "You curled your finger."

Jake stared at his hand. Lauren could tell he was concentrating, forcing his mind to order his hand to move.

"Don't force it. You know it doesn't work that way. But you are healing. It was a small movement. The important thing is it happened. Maybe you should have an EMG."

"A what?"

"Electromyography. A diagnostic procedure to assess the health of muscles and nerves."

"How would you know that's significant or how it works?" he asked.

Lauren felt her face grow hot. She'd made a mistake. Had she revealed her training? "When I took this job, I checked out your condition on the internet."

He frowned. "That doesn't give you everything."

"It was enough for me to know a little bit about how such injuries work. I don't claim to be an expert, but I wanted to be able to help if I could."

He seemed to accept that.

"You should probably see your doctor and let him or her know this happened."

"You'll have to come with me."

"Why?"

"Because I didn't see it happen. You'll need to answer all the questions."

"This seems like something a parent or wife would do. I'm not related to you."

"I'm an adult," he said. "I have the right to allow you access if I wish."

Of course, that was true, Lauren knew. She was used to dealing with parents, having them explain symptoms to her because their child had a problem answering questions. Some kids were shy, some afraid, but she didn't think she'd end up in a doctor's office giving the details of what had happened to Jake.

"I don't have much to say," she said. "You should see a doctor and request another appointment to have them check for muscle activity."

Jake frowned at the word *doctor*. Lauren

remembered Cal's comment on how his brother refused to see any more doctors.

"If I agree to go with you, will you make the appointment?"

He hesitated a long time. "Maybe."

"What is it?" Lauren asked. "Other than a dentist, you haven't been to a doctor. You are a doctor, so if you can get help, why won't you take it?"

"Suppose it doesn't work?"

"Suppose what doesn't work? You aren't going there to find something that works. You want to know the progress, the status."

"I want hope," he said.

Lauren stopped. How could she not see that this conversation was heading in that direction?

"I want to be assured that something positive will happen as a result, that I will get the use of my arm back. I want to know that I'll be able to tie my shoes and hug a woman with both hands. Going to another doctor and finding out nothing has changed takes my hope away."

"Is that what you feel you did to patients?"

"Sometimes. There comes a time when

there is nothing medicine can do. I had to tell the patients."

"How often did you do that? I mean, were you giving hope more than taking it away?"

He thought a moment, then said, "It was more giving hope. While some patients' problems weren't totally corrected, they had hope that someday they would be."

"Jake," she said quietly. "So do you."

She wrapped her fingers around his, alert for movement, but nothing happened. When she looked up, Jake's eyes were on her.

"See what I mean?" he asked.

Their faces were close to each other. Lauren reached up and smoothed the frown from his brow. "Isn't it better to know than not know?" she whispered.

"I guess it's better to know."

The look that Jake gave her nearly burned. Lauren knew he wasn't talking about his paralysis. He took her hand and pulled her closer.

"Jake," she said, her voice full of emotion.

"I need to know," he said and kissed her.

JAKE DIDN'T KNOW how to begin. Lauren had known right away that there had been a woman in his life. After the accident, Jake tried to put her out of his mind, but it didn't work. He'd gone through scenario after scenario about that day. If he hadn't gone to Europe. If he'd stayed at the hotel for lunch. If he hadn't run across the street against the light, he'd have been several yards behind the explosion. The concussive force of the impact might have knocked him down, but it wouldn't have had the devastating effect on his arm and hand that it did.

"Jake."

Lauren's voice was soft, almost a whisper when she called his name. It was uncanny how she could read his moods and try not to intrude on them, while also bringing him out of any introspection that she deemed unhealthy.

"What are you thinking?"

Lauren didn't talk in riddles or offer rationalizations. She was clear and direct.

"Dance with me," he said.

She looked around the room. They were in the windows room. She called it that sometimes and Jake had begun to think of it the same way.

"There's no music."

Taking out his phone, he pushed a few buttons and music filled the air. Jake opened his arm and Lauren stepped forward. He slowly waltzed her about the room, avoiding the furniture.

When the song ended, another began.

"Her name was Jennifer," Jake began.

Lauren didn't move in his arm. She said nothing and Jake understood that she knew who he meant.

"We met during a sailing competition. I was on a crew team. We'd been challenged by a rival team and were gathered on the lake. I don't remember if Jennifer came with anyone, but we left together and from then on we were rarely without one another."

They were no longer moving about the floor, no longer dancing, just turning around and around in the same place.

"We were engaged. I thought I was what she wanted. We had fun together, but we'd never talked about the important things that a marriage meant, children, careers, hopes and dreams. Then the accident happened."

Their steps stalled, but the two of them didn't part. Lauren looked at him. Her eyes seemed huge this close to him. "What happened?" she whispered.

"She stayed around while I was in the hospital, but when she found I couldn't use my arm or hand, she ended our engagement. She said she couldn't take care of an invalid. She didn't want the kind of life that would entail for us now."

Lauren gasped. "I'm so sorry."

"It was for the best in the long run," he said. And now he believed it. "She was honest, at least. I wished her well in the end."

"You must have been heartbroken," Lauren said.

"I thought I was. There was so much on my plate at the time that it was difficult to separate one emotion from another."

When Jake sorted them out, Jennifer was the least of his worries. He put her out of his life, but both he and Cal knew that the experience had soured him for another relationship. No one, however, had prepared him for a kindergarten teacher with the ability to massage the pain from his arm and talk his ear off.

Or worm her way into his frozen heart and cause it to thaw.

"The music stopped," Lauren said.

Jake realized the song ended minutes ago, yet they stood in the dance position like two statues watching darkness fall.

"Do you want children?" Lauren asked.

Jake hadn't thought about that. Cal was unmarried. They had cousins who had kids, but few that they spent any amount of time with.

Jake dropped his arm, but took her hand. He led her to the sofa and they sat down.

"I had never thought of children of my own. The only child I would think of is the one on the operating table. Since the accident, I've had time to think about Cal and my life when we were young, the things we did with our parents, vacations we took, places we explored."

"That's where you get your adventurous spirit," Lauren said.

"I suppose. You wouldn't think so. My mother was a nurse and my father a mathematician. He was the one who went on the adventures with us. If I was a father, I'd like to be like him."

"That's a wonderful story," she said. After

a long pause she asked, "What about careers, hopes and dreams?"

"They're still to be determined. I am a doctor," he said. "I haven't said that in a while. I haven't even thought of it."

"That's your career. What about hopes and dreams?"

"Those are hard to put into words. One day I hope to explain them to you."

"But not now," she said.

He shook his head. "There's a lot I still have to work out before I can tell you what they are."

"I'll hold you to that," she said.

THE DREAM. LAUREN STOPPED abruptly as she pulled a T-shirt over her head. She suddenly remembered last night's dream. She didn't often remember her dreams and she was grateful for that. After Naliani, Lauren was plagued with nightmares of her daughter and the Herculean effort Lauren had tried to use to save her. No matter what, the result was always the same. Naliani died. Lauren would wake shaking, her heart hammering and her body drenched in sweat.

This dream wasn't like that. It was her

birthday and all her friends were running around the yard at her family's Maryland home. She was ten and about to open her presents. The one she was holding was from her father. He smiled at her and she felt loved and safe. She pulled the ribbon on the box and then everything disappeared as she woke up.

Where did that come from? Lauren asked herself. She went back to dressing, but the dream didn't leave her memory now. Where was her mother in the dream? She should have been there. Lauren didn't know and didn't remember where she was at that exact moment. Maybe she was in the house or taking a picture.

Lauren finished brushing her hair and left the room to head downstairs. Jake looked up from the first floor and her thoughts shifted to him.

"What are we going to do today?" he asked. His voice was jovial and Lauren felt like it was going to be a good day.

She ran down the stairs and accepted the cup of coffee he was holding.

"You're up early," she said. Lauren was

usually on her second cup of coffee before Jake appeared. "What do you want to do?"

"Well, since we were successful the last time, why don't we get in the car and see where the road leads us."

That's what they did. When they reached the halfway point on the New Jersey Turnpike and Jake hadn't taken any exit, Lauren asked where they were going.

"How about we go to Washington, DC?"

"What?" It was the last place she expected. "That's two hundred miles from here. We'd have to stay overnight."

"We could, but I've done it in one day. Go down in the morning, like now. And come back at midnight."

"We wouldn't get back until four o'clock in the morning."

"We can sleep in tomorrow."

Lauren was lost for an argument. He was right. There was no reason they couldn't go to the capital. It's not like either of them had a job to get back to. If Jake needed to consult, he could do it from a hotel's business center or a library.

"What are we going to do when we get

there? Most of the monuments require tickets that have to be obtained in advance."

"Even if all we do is walk around, it'll be worth it. When was the last time you were there?"

"Not for years," Lauren said, watching the miles fly by.

When they reached the city, they left the car in a garage.

"From here on, we're on foot," Jake said.

"Obviously you're very familiar with this city."

"I've spent some time here," he said. "And while there are new buildings going up all the time, most of the square miles remain the same.

It was always humid in Washington in the summer and this day was no different. Lauren wore a T-shirt and shorts. They bought hot dogs and drinks from a street vendor, then walked across the mall and sat down on the grass to admire the scene.

"We could have done this in Central Park," Jake said. "But this is different."

"It is," Lauren smiled.

"I know it was a surprise when I said we should come here."

"I'm sure you had another reason than just going for a long ride."

He laughed. She knew him so well. "I spent a couple of summers here after I got out of medical school, met some friends, did some outrageously stupid things." He laughed remembering some of the foolish things they'd gotten up to.

"Like what?" Lauren finished the last of her hot dog and stared at him.

"Nothing like college students are doing today. Our antics are tame compared to theirs. We used to go to Dupont Circle and run lines of people across the circle and then around it just as the traffic started to build."

"You could have gotten killed."

"Not when you think you've got the world at your feet."

Jake hadn't intended to, but he looked at his arm, a sharp reminder of how fragile our bodies really were.

"Glad you made it to twenty-three," she said.

Jake stood up and offered her his hand. She took it and he helped her to her feet. Slipping her own hand through his arm, they started walking toward the Lincoln Memorial.

"No tickets required for this one," he told her.

They spent most of the day walking. When they were tired or weak from the humidity, they'd grab a drink from one of the many vendors and take a seat in the park. By dinnertime they were in Georgetown.

"There used to be a trolley that ran here," Jake said. "Some of the tracks are still in the street." Lauren looked where he pointed.

They went in and out of the many shops that Georgetown was known for.

"We should get something to eat and head back," Lauren said.

The sun had begun to set and it would be dark soon. "We could stay the night and drive back tomorrow," Jake suggested.

Lauren frowned, but he could tell she was considering it.

"How about it? Then we could have a long, leisurely dinner and not worry about driving in the dark."

"This from a man who used to run out in traffic just to stop the cars."

"That man has more sense now."

"All right. I'll see if I can make us a reservation somewhere."

"No need," Jake said. "It's already done."

"What?" Her eyebrows rose.

"Just in case," he said.

"You had this planned all along," Lauren accused.

"No more so than a picnic that was really a driving lesson."

They both laughed.

Jake had booked them each a suite at the Mayflower Hotel. When he met Lauren for dinner, she was no longer wearing a T-shirt and shorts. She turned totally around, showing off a yellow sundress and matching shoes.

"You clean up well," he said. "I'm glad the hotel shop had something that nice for you."

"You clean up well, too."

Jake had obviously done the same. He no longer had on the same clothes. The hotel's men's shop had accommodated him with dress slacks and a shirt.

They ate dinner at a restaurant directly next to the river. The display of lights outside and across the water was spectacular. Ambient light filtered in from the window, setting fire to the reddish highlights of Lauren's hair. It couldn't have been more perfect if a Hollywood expert had crafted the scene. Jake had often watched her in the waning light of the setting sun in his apartment. It was perfect for her.

And perfect for him.

CHAPTER TEN

HE AND LAUREN returned from Washington the next day. They didn't leave in the morning, but spent part of the day visiting the tourist attractions. Jake, who thought he hated tourists, didn't even notice them when he was with Lauren. She was like a kid, experiencing Christmas for the first time.

They'd meandered through some stores and she bought a slew of specialty papers, paintbrushes and small pots of paint and children's books. When asked what it was for, she would say only, "You'll see." Jake hadn't seen anything yet.

Alone in the apartment, he was missing Lauren. Then his phone rang.

"Hello," Jake said, elongating the word in a slightly silly way. Seeing Cal's name on his phone, he muted the television.

"Wow," Cal's voice came through the receiver. "You sound happy. What's going on?"

Jake heard the surprise in his brother's voice.

"Nothing. I was watching something on television that was funny."

"You're watching television?" Cal asked. "The last time I remember you watching television there was a purple dinosaur that sang."

Jake laughed. "Probably. Lately Lauren and I watch movies to relax."

"Lauren and I?" The question in Cal's voice was obvious.

"Don't jump to conclusions," Jake warned.

"I'm not jumping. I can hear it in your voice. You like Lauren. Is she there with you now?"

"I'm alone. It's her day off."

Most of the time, Lauren remained in the apartment or told him where she was going, but today she was gone when he got up. She had her cell phone number, so he could reach her if necessary. He missed her and had come in to watch television and wait for her to return. He also tried to move his arm. He was always trying to move it, but it never cooperated.

Watching the comedy show had taken his

mind off his arm. Nothing could remove thoughts of Lauren from his brain.

"So you do like her," Cal stated. "That's great. I'm glad you're interested in a woman again."

"I never said that."

"You don't have to. It's in your voice. Even through the phone, I can hear it. How does she feel about you?"

Jake remembered her touch. He remembered the couple of times he'd kissed her and he remembered all the little things she did for him: massaging his arm, dancing with him by the light of the city outside the windows, playing tennis, having a picnic.

"She has some affection for me. I'm not sure how deep it goes," Jake said.

"Have you told her how you feel?"

Jake realized his brother had already jumped over the hurdle that said *relationship*.

"Are you putting obstacles in the way?" Cal asked before Jake could reply. "Wondering if spending time with Lauren will end the same way it did with your ex-fiancée?"

"It's crossed my mind, but Lauren is nothing like Jennifer."

It wasn't that Jake didn't have reservations in the back of his mind. Jennifer couldn't deal with his injury and Lauren approached it head-on.

"Is she in it for the long haul?" Cal asked. "When I hired her, she said it was temporary."

"She's promised to remain until you return."

"That could be a long while," Cal said.

"I'm sure she'll make a decision about her future and if she needs to remain here any longer."

"Does that mean you're ready to return to the hospital and—"

"No," Jake cut him off.

"The longer you wait, the worse it could be."

Jake knew that. He also knew that in the last two years, the prognosis he received was the same every time; the illness was psychosomatic. He had been to the doctor with Lauren. After she told him he'd moved his finger in the theater. He kept that from Cal. His brother would jump on the tiny phantom movement as if Jake had climbed Mount Whitney. Then he'd insist he continue to see doctors. Lauren had done that once, and she'd accepted their report. It was time Cal did the same.

THE BALL FLEW over the net and hit the court at Jake's feet. "Hey, you're getting good at this," he called to Lauren. Her shots were inconsistent. Often they didn't hit the mark, but one in a million was right on point.

"So are you."

Jake had to admit, he never thought Lauren's idea of him participating in a sport would ever work. But in her usual fashion she was right. At first, his left-handed strokes were a bust, but she persisted and he could almost focus on the placement of his shots.

They played every morning at a private club where Jake was a member. At first they would arrive early, before the fitness crowd came in. Then it was before breakfast. Jake endured the gawkers, people staring at him. Lauren spun it, letting him know they were fascinated by his ability to play with only one hand. Jake understood what she was saying, accepted it and turned the tables by waving at his audience.

Eventually, he and Lauren became familiar to the crowd and the gawking stopped.

"Remember what I told you," he shouted to Lauren. "Stand sideways when you swing at the ball and follow through over your shoulder."

She nodded and when he sent her a soft ball, it came back hard and in the court. Jake's head whipped around to see where the ball landed. Lauren was jumping up and down, celebrating that she'd done something right. If he was really coaching her, he'd tell her to save her celebration until the point was totally over, but she looked like a child with a new puppy, and he wouldn't take that away from her.

They worked for another hour and Lauren said she was tired. The truth was she was letting him know his exercise period was over for the day. It was a good workout and Jake felt great afterward. Except for her having to tie his shoes, he loved everything about their tennis game.

He even enjoyed teaching, something he never thought he'd like. He was a participant, rather than thinking he'd merely be on the sidelines. Lauren was definitely the raw student. She'd never held a racquet and he could show her the right way to play, but he wasn't a trained instructor. Still, she was an excellent pupil.

He looked at his arm. He didn't think that was going to happen anytime soon, but on the positive side—and Lauren continually told him to look at the positives—he was developing a technique with his left hand that could work for recreational play.

Jake counted himself lucky—another positive—that he'd run into her on the street that day. Where would he be now if she had just picked up her packages and rushed off? He guessed he could thank the universe for them colliding at just that moment.

"Good workout," she said, a little winded, as she joined him. They walked toward the common area of the tennis club. There was no set rule as to which of them drove back to the apartment. There they often showered, dressed and had breakfast before going out for the day.

Jake loved that the days were no longer routine. They played tennis together and he did video consultations, but for the most part each day was different. He could thank only Lauren for that.

Jake was going to have to think of something he could do for her.

LAUREN STAMPED HER foot as her tennis ball pitched into the net. She thought she'd be better after a week of trying to follow instructions.

"What am I doing wrong?" she shouted across the net. They'd been playing for nearly half an hour and most of her balls were mishits, flying this way and that off the court.

Jake walked to the net. With his racket in his left hand, he waved Lauren forward. "You need to keep your feet moving." He demonstrated holding the racket in the ready position and showing her how to move her body.

"I thought I was doing that."

"You were, but then you turned back." Again, he demonstrated. "Your feet and body should be like this." His side was facing the net. "What you're doing is beginning this way, then turning to face the net. When you do that, it's harder to hit the ball."

Lauren nodded. "I'll try to remember that, along with all the other things I have to remember."

They hadn't played any matches yet. Her goal was to get the ball back across the net and to keep Jake active.

Jake smiled apologetically. Lauren returned to the baseline muttering all the instructions Jake had taught her.

When she was in place again, Jake hit a ball to her. Lauren let it bounce, then swung.

"Great form," Jake called.

"I still missed the ball," she complained.

Her timing was off. The ball was already behind her when she swung at it.

"You'll get it. Patience, remember?"

Lauren wiped the sweat from her forehead with the sweatband on her wrist and stood ready for the next shot. Jake hit balls to her and she tried to return them. Only a couple landed on his side of the net.

"Tired?" he asked as they passed each other changing court position.

"Not yet."

She had to be tired. But Lauren wasn't one to give up. Jake had learned that about her. They each had a long drink of water and began again. While he wasn't ambidextrous and wasn't even close to his previous ability, he appreciated what he'd achieved so far, and enjoyed watching the teens. He also got a lot of pleasure in seeing Lauren trying something new.

They resumed playing. Time flew by.

"Last ball," Jake called.

Lauren bounced the ball and hit it softly. She'd been hitting hard, fast balls and this soft one threw him. Jake lunged for it and missed. Lauren smiled and jumped for joy.

Jake knew she'd been imitating him. Her decision to change things up was a great strategy. He should have suggested it to her, but he was too used to winning.

Jake smiled at the exuberance. It was only a game, but her reaction was that of someone who'd won the US Open. He couldn't help laughing. He remembered his first win and knew exactly how she felt.

Her effort could carry her through the rest of the week. Then she started to run toward the net. Jake quickly saw what she intended and he knew it was a bad idea. He started forward. The net was higher than most people thought it was. Even at its center it was thirty-six inches high, three inches higher than a woman's hurdle. She might clear it, but more people than not had been injured trying to jump over the net.

Lauren was already in the air before he got close enough to stop her. Dropping the racket he still carried, he raised his left arm to try to catch her. It was a useless thing to do. He knew that, but his arm was in the air before his mind was fully engaged. Jake saw her front foot clear the net, but her back foot clipped the tape and she started to fall. She crashed into him. Her weight and the momentum of her leap overbalanced him. They fell toward the court. He was quick to keep his head from making contact with the surface as they slid several feet.

"Are you all right?" Lauren asked, her voice winded, her face flushed. Tendrils of hair that had escaped her ponytail tickled his cheek.

Jake started to laugh. "You are the one who nearly broke your neck and you're asking how I am?"

Lauren slid off Jake and they sat up. "I'm sorry," she said. "I didn't mean to…"

"It's all right. Neither of us is hurt."

"I won't try that again," she said.

"Good."

Jake stood up and offered Lauren his hand. She took it. He felt the warmth of her fingers as he pulled her to her feet. Jake quickly checked her arms and legs for scrapes or scratches. She'd fallen into him and he'd taken the brunt of the impact.

"I'm not usually an impulsive person," Lauren said. "I didn't even think about not making the jump."

Jake listened. He knew what she meant. She was happy and he didn't want to destroy the moment by explaining how badly she could have been hurt.

"How about we call it a day and go celebrate with a glass of orange juice?"

"I'd like that."

The orange juice came with a full breakfast and a walk through Central Park. Months ago Jake would never have thought he'd be out of his apartment. He certainly didn't think he'd have a woman at his side who didn't judge him or look at his arm as an infirmity. He pressed Lauren's hold on him a little tighter. She looked up and smiled.

They didn't speak. Jake found there were times when conversation wasn't necessary for communication. He'd never known anyone like her or anyone he was so comfortable with. She did protect him, however. She shielded him from onlookers who would become conscious of his hand. Jake was used to being the protector, but Lauren was able to look after him without putting him in a position of need. If she wasn't a kindergarten teacher, her calling had to be in medical rehabilitation. But she didn't just heal the body. Her expertise was in making someone see the possible roads that were open to them even if one path was blocked.

Jake dropped his arm and entwined his fingers with Lauren's. She looked at their hands, then up at him. He smiled. And there was that communication he felt. No words. No gestures. Just understanding.

JAKE'S EYES JERKED open and he sat up in bed as if propelled from behind. The sound woke him and he realized he'd shouted out in his sleep. His heart pounded and his body was drenched in sweat. Immediately, he went hot, then cold. Leaning over the side of the bed, he sat up, hanging his head in his hand. It had been a dream. Relief flooded his mind, but his body pumped fear and disbelief.

In his dream, he hadn't caught Lauren as her foot hit the tennis net. There was no net. They weren't in a tennis facility. They were outside in a field with a rope tied between two trees. On the rope was a collection of dresses. He recognized the princess one. The ground under them sported a blanket with a picnic basket.

Lauren ran toward him. Just as he'd known what she was going to do on the tennis court, he knew her intentions about the rope. He was too far away to reach her as she became airborne, although he ran as hard as he could to reach her. The dream slowed his actions, making him feel as if he was moving in slow motion, fighting the air, cutting through it as if it was tangible. Her shoe connected with the mermaid's costume hanging on the rope. It triggered a bomb. The explosion grabbed him with an invisible hand, pushed him back, lifted his body from the ground and forced it through the thick air before dropping him onto the grassy ground.

Jake looked at the floor, refusing to close his eyes in case the dream returned. He breathed in hard, sucking air into his lungs and forcing it out long and slow. It was only a dream, he told himself, a nightmare that had been jumbled up with the memories of the terrorist attack that had damaged his arm.

He knew lying down and going back to sleep would be fruitless, at least for the next few hours. Needing something cold to drink, he stood up and rolled his shoulders. He stretched as he walked. Then he went down the stairs heading for the kitchen.

"Jake."

He looked back and saw Lauren with her hands on the railing.

"Are you all right? I heard you call out."

"It was nothing. I had a bad dream," he said. He knew Lauren would keep at him until he told her why he was out of bed in the middle of the night, but he didn't want to give her the cold truth.

She came down the stairs, her robe flowing behind her.

"I was going to get a drink."

Jake went in the kitchen, returning with two glasses of water.

"Tell me about it," Lauren said.

She used her teacher's voice. Yet Jake had no intention of giving her the details of the dream. He drank the bottle of water almost to the bottom. "It wasn't about anything really. I hardly remember it."

"Sit down," Lauren said.

Following her instruction, he sat. She moved behind him. Soft music began to play from the concealed speakers in the wall. Without him asking, Lauren approached him and started to massage his arm. He hadn't felt any pain in it in weeks. Tonight the hurt returned and she must have read the expression on his face or seen something in his walk that told her he needed the magic of her hands.

Jake let her work in silence. Her hands were warm as she found the exact place where the pain culminated and eased it away. Not for the first time, Jake wondered how she could be so intuitive and how she knew exactly where to work on his pain. Too bad she couldn't make his nightmares vanish.

"You have a lot more muscle definition now," she said.

"All that tennis and walking and picnicking," he laughed, but it didn't feel mirthful. Jake was still in the clutches of the nightmare, although Lauren's hands were soothing.

"Talk to me, Jake," she said.

He didn't need to ask what she meant. Jake took a moment before beginning. He used the time to think of what he wanted to say. "The nightmare was about the tennis game we played."

Her fingers stopped moving. "The one where I won?"

He didn't want to take the pleasure he remembered her feeling away. "Not that one, another one."

"What happened?" Lauren resumed her massage.

"A bomb went off."

"Was I hurt?" she asked.

Jake jerked around to look at her, the pain in his back and shoulder forgotten. "I never said you were in it."

"But I was, wasn't I?"

He nodded.

"Was I hurt?" she asked again.

"Yes," he stated.

"And you tried to save me."

"I was too late," Jake said. "The bomb went off while I was trying to get to you. The impact of the force pushed me back. That's when I woke up."

Jake realized that, with only a few alterations, Lauren had guessed what happened to him on that Paris street.

"How do you feel about it?"

He turned back and she again started to knead the tension out of his muscles.

"I was afraid for you."

"Thank you for caring," she said.

Lauren stopped and moved around to sit next to him. The music still played in the background, but he hadn't been paying any attention to it. Now he heard the soft sounds of violins and horns. He knew the song, but couldn't place the title just then.

"Dance with me?" he suddenly asked Lauren.

"What?"

Jake stood and looked down to see the confusion in her eyes. He offered his hand and she took it, standing up. Jake wasn't wearing his sling. He didn't sleep in it. Lauren took his right hand and placed it behind her back. They began swaying to the music.

Jake wanted to distract her from the dream, but he was being distracted now. One song ended, but he didn't stop the dance. As another one began, they continued to move together.

"Your dancing has improved too," Lauren said.

Her head reached his chin and Jake felt her smile. He drew her closer and they continued to circle the room. Two other songs ended while they danced in the darkened morning.

"Jake," Lauren whispered. Her voice was soft and sexy. "Do you feel anything?"

He pushed her back and looked into her face. Her eyes were wide and bright and beautiful.

"Is that a trick question or just a loaded one?" he asked. "Of course I feel something."

Jake kissed her. He liked holding her, even if she was aware of everything about him and wouldn't allow him to hide behind his pain.

Lauren's head rested on his shoulder after

they kissed. He kept her close, savoring the moment.

"That's not what I meant," she told him, although her voice was thick with emotion. "Your arm is pressing me to you."

Immediately, all the strength he'd been using was gone. His arm fell to his side as if it suddenly remembered it had no feeling. Jake released Lauren and looked at his limp arm.

Turning away from her, he took several steps. "Why do you do this to me?" he shouted, frustration clear in his voice.

"What?" Lauren asked.

"Not you. It's…" He sat down on the sofa, tipped his head back to stare at the ceiling. "Me, the universe, the forces that be." His gaze landed on Lauren.

"Jake, it's a sign. You're getting feeling back in your arm. Eventually, it's going to move. I'm sure of it."

"You more than me."

"Jake?" Lauren said quietly as if something had just occurred to her. "Has this happened before? You asked why this happens to you as if this wasn't the first time you've gone through it."

He sighed. "I didn't want to tell you."

"How many times?"

"Two, other than just now. It's usually while I'm asleep. I wake up with a tingling in my hand."

"That's good. Why didn't you want to tell me?"

"You're so optimistic. You assume everything will work out for me. If I let you know I had a tingling in my finger, you'd have me back at a doctor's office and I'm not going."

"I want to say I wouldn't have done that. But I know I'd have insisted that you try to find out if anything was happening. You're a doctor. You know that it's better to listen to your body than to allow it to make decisions for you."

"I am a doctor and I know that they won't find anything this time, exactly like they found nothing the last time. If feeling is going to return, it will do it when it's ready."

"But you don't put much store in that."

He dropped his shoulders and shook his head.

"Well, I do," Lauren said. "All the signs are there and they are happening more often."

"Stop!" Jake shouted so loud Lauren jumped

back. He relaxed a moment and spoke in a lower voice. "I'm sorry. I didn't mean to yell."

"All right, Jake, no doctors for now. But would you think about it? We've gone to the doctor before. If these episodes keep happening, something is either working or getting worse. You need to find out which."

"I promise to think about it." He would, but he no longer wanted to discuss this now.

"Thanks," Lauren said. "Would you at least let me check your arm?"

"No," he said, witnessing the expected surprise on her face. "If you touch me, I'm going to kiss you again."

"And neither one of us wants that kind of complication," she finished for him.

CHAPTER ELEVEN

DAYS PAST AND Jake still hadn't called a doctor. He'd tried every day, several times a day, to move his arm, but nothing happened. He didn't doubt that Lauren thought she had felt the pressure at her back while they danced, and yet… Had she imagined it, wanted to see him get better? He felt her heart was in the right place, that she truly wanted him to regain the use of his arm and hand, but she also forced him to see that he had another avenue to go to if plan A failed.

Jake spoke to the hospital every day. He hadn't mentioned Lauren's observation to anyone. Once he'd been tempted at the end of the call, but at the last minute he decided against it. Fear and the possibility of hopelessness paralyzed him as much as the inability to use his arm. There was one point when he thought he could move it, the first time

Lauren took his arm. He was sure he could pull away from her. But it didn't happen.

"Good morning," Lauren said as she entered the kitchen. "I could smell the coffee." After pouring herself a cup, she sat opposite him and slid a piece of paper across the table.

"What's this?"

"These are the tests you're about to have for your arm and hand. You didn't make an appointment, so I talked to Dr. Chase and made one for you."

"You had no right."

"I'm more than a friend, so I gave myself the right. I wouldn't let you drive drunk, so I won't let you atrophy if you don't need to."

Jake looked at the list. CT scan, MRI, myelography and electromyography.

"Since you already have a baseline, they can compare the new tests and see if there is a change."

"I just went to a doctor not that long ago. I don't need to go again."

"Haven't we already had this conversation?" she asked. "You agreed to go if I'd go with you. So, we're going."

She made it sound final. Jake wasn't convinced. He'd been through this before and nothing good ever came of it.

"When is this appointment?"

"Tomorrow morning, nine o'clock."

"How'd you get one so quickly? These usually take months if it isn't an emergency."

"You underestimate your status in the medical community. They were glad to fit you in."

Jake knew fighting with her was a waste of time. If she had to, she'd hire orderlies to strong-arm him and carry him to the doctor's office. He may as well go. What could one more appointment reveal, tests or no tests? And then Lauren would know that her efforts were fruitless. He had to give her credit for trying. For someone who'd never been a companion, she took very good care of him. He almost laughed when he saw the list of tests. Dr. Chase must have explained the terms *myelography* and *electromyography*. Lauren had even pronounced them correctly.

"All right, Doctor." He said the word sarcastically. She was acting like she knew what she was talking about. "I'll go, but don't expect anything new to come from this."

"At least it'll keep your mind from gnawing at you that something might be happening. You'll keep trying to move your arm every day and if still nothing happens, it'll eat at you until you retreat to that bed again."

Jake had tried to move his arm and hand, that was true. He'd spoken to both out loud and willed either to move just a centimeter. He wanted some sort of validation that what Lauren had seen and felt was real. But nothing happened.

Jake stood up, taking his coffee cup with him. He leaned against the refrigerator and stared at Lauren.

"What?" she finally asked.

"Your ex called you Lori," he stated.

"It's a shortened version of Lauren," she admitted.

"How about Graves? Is that a shortened version of Peterson?"

Lauren's cup stopped halfway to the table.

"You're Lori Graves. We went to college together."

"I didn't think you even knew my name back then," she said.

"I didn't. But the night your ex-husband called you Lori, I remembered why I thought you looked familiar. But you've changed. You wore your hair in a long ponytail back then. And you hardly ever said a word."

"It was a bad hair year," she said.

"My yearbooks are in storage, but I accessed one online and found a photo of you. Under the without-a-smile face was the name Lauren Graves."

"I was Lauren Graves. When I married I took Richard's last name."

"Why didn't you tell me you knew who I was when you first came?" Jake asked.

"Do you remember our first encounter in this apartment?"

He nodded. "I hardly gave you time to say much."

"Between trying to get me to leave and ignoring me, how could I say, 'By the way, I sat a couple of rows behind you in physics class during college'?"

"Physics." Jake returned to the table and sat down. "How did you become a kindergarten teacher when you were in physics?"

"That wasn't my major."

"Then why did you take it?"

She looked down and up again. "I was

interested in someone in the class. He was enrolled, so I enrolled too."

Jake smiled. "I suppose we've all done something like that. What happened? Did you two date?"

She shook her head. "I lost track of him after graduation."

"But you met someone else."

"And you will too," she answered.

Jake almost blurted that he wouldn't. He'd gone down that road once and while he'd truly like to get to know Lauren better, he wasn't thinking of ever marrying. Not after his last fiasco with Jennifer.

"Someone I can call by a pet name?" he asked.

She smiled. Jake didn't like it. Was she thinking of her ex?

"You're not planning to call me Lori, right?"

"I wouldn't dream of it." He didn't tell her the name he would dream of.

"JAKE, I'M BACK," Lauren called. She'd been out running errands. Jake didn't respond. She checked the kitchen, then the media room. Jake wasn't in either, but there was a book lying on the sofa.

She dropped her packages and stepped over to look at it. Catholic University's yearbook lay closed on the sofa. Feelings of loyalty and past friendships during her college years flooded her memory. Her alma mater. Hers and Jake's. Sitting down, she picked up the heavy tome and laid it across her lap. The book was from her junior year. Jake would have been a senior. She started to flip the pages, curious to see his younger face. She noticed a card acting as a bookmark. Opening to that page, she gazed at the two-page spread and smiled.

"You found it," Jake said, coming into the room.

"You went to the trouble of getting this out of storage?" she asked, glancing up at him and then down at the book, opened to an arrangement of color photos and students' names under each one.

Jake took a seat, but said nothing.

Lauren giggled. She saw the picture of herself with a group of students from the biology club. Lauren thought about that girl, tall, lanky, all arms and legs. While other girls walked as if they'd had modeling classes, Lauren was a fish in a jungle; lost, out of place, trying to find where she fit in the scheme of things. Thankfully, she found it with the biology club.

"Look how young and pretty you are." His shoulder brushed hers as he leaned forward to point at her sitting in the center of the photo.

"I haven't seen pictures like this in years."

"We were talking the other morning about being at the same college. So I went to find the actual yearbook. I couldn't remember us being in a class together."

"You wouldn't," Lauren teased.

"And why is that?"

"You were a BMOC. Everyone knows a big man on campus. You excelled in everything. You were handsome, intelligent, great at sports and always surrounded by beautiful women. Do you think with all that glamour you'd even notice her?"

She pointed to her own photo. Her bangs were too long, although her flyaway hair had been brushed and sprayed for the photo.

Jake didn't answer her question, but posed

another one. "What was your major? This is a biology club. Weren't you in education?"

She shook her head. "Biology was my major."

"Did you plan to teach it?"

Lauren turned the pages, looking for a photo that had Jake in it.

"I planned to go to medical school," she said. Lauren knew it was better to stick to as much of the truth as she could.

"What happened?"

She looked down again at the pages of the yearbook. She turned several of them intent on finding photos of Jake.

"Lauren?" he prompted.

"Tuition and fees," she said. "I thought I'd work for a while, earn the money and apply later. Then I was married and I had Naliani."

She left it at that. The sequence was wrong, but she couldn't tell Jake that.

Not yet.

She found a photo. "Look at you." She knew she sounded a little excited. Jake was on the track field, totally airborne as he cleared a hurdle. Lauren compared the younger Jake with the man he was now. He'd gotten more handsome with age. The nineteen-year-old was still angular. While Jake had mellowed over the years, he had a worldliness about him in the photo. His experience and maturity showed.

And Lauren liked it. The first time she saw him, she thought he was the most striking guy she'd ever seen. The years between college and now had been more than kind to him. He was even better-looking today than he was back in college.

Jake frowned at another photo of himself, this one in a classroom. "I should have had a haircut."

"You didn't know they were going to take a photo that day." Jake was in the third desk closest to the windows. Lauren didn't know what the subject was since there was no board. Books were open on desks, but she couldn't tell what subject they covered.

The photography club often took photos for their classes, the school paper or the yearbook. This looked like one of those. As a rule, they snapped a disproportionate number of photos of the popular campus students, Jake being one.

"What was it like for you in college?"

Lauren smiled. "I had my share of parties, dances and being too tired to go to class after a long night. For the most part, I enjoyed it."

"You were the loved-to-learn type, I bet."

"As were you," she threw at him. Flipping the pages back to the beginning, she again looked at the photo of a nineteen-year-old Jake. "Remember him?" Lauren pointed to the picture.

"He was an arrogant kid."

"Doctor in the making," she said.

LAUREN SCANNED THE list of doctors in the wing of the hospital where she and Jake waited. She sighed with relief when she didn't see any name she knew. Jake looked stoic. She knew he didn't want to be here and she tried to make jokes or talk to him to get him to relax. He was having none of it.

Finally, in the waiting room, she took his hand. While it didn't respond to her touch, the action seemed to have a calming effect on him. It was short-lived. As soon as the nurse came out and called his name, he tensed. Taking a moment to breathe, he stood up.

"I'll be right here when you come out," she said.

"You're going with me. This was your idea. You can see it through."

Lauren stood and the two went through the door into the labyrinth of back corridors of the hospital. Jake was shuttled from room to room. Doctors and technicians massaged, probed and tested various levels of activity in his muscles. They moved his right arm and hand, rotating them up and down and opening and closing his fingers. They asked Jake to try to move both his hand and arm himself. Nothing happened.

In another room, Lauren watched as a technician slid Jake, who was lying on a large table, into the cylindrical scanner of an MRI machine. After that, he was taken for the electromyography. This was the test Lauren was most interested in. It could help diagnose or exclude muscle disorders, those that affected the motor neurons in the brain or spinal cord, and nerve roots.

The thing none of the tests could determine was Jake's will to use his hand. While these tests would rule out any medical condition preventing his movement, they did nothing to explain any underlying psychological reasons preventing his movement.

Most people having medical tests considered it a slow process since it could take days or weeks for the results. It was stressful for the patient and, in Lauren's case, the parents. Dr. Chase said he'd fast-track the results as much as he could and give Jake a call. After that, Jake couldn't get out of the hospital fast enough.

Jake practically sprinted to the car. Good thing for Lauren, since she saw a colleague she knew and stopped to say hello. Her eyes darted back and forth to Jake to make sure he didn't double back and ask to be introduced. Lauren finished her conversation and headed for the car. Jake was already in the passenger seat.

The trip back to the apartment was made in silence. Lauren searched for something to say, but not talking seemed the better decision. She kept quiet until they were inside the apartment.

"Are you going to sulk for the rest of the day?" she asked.

"I do not sulk," he said.

"Then what is your definition for your attitude?"

"I told you it was a waste of time."

"You don't know that, at least not yet. Wait for the test results."

"I'm a doctor. I know," he said.

"If you're a doctor, why haven't you healed yourself?"

He turned away from her, offering his silent back. Inwardly, Lauren flinched. She could tell that she'd touched a live nerve and he didn't like it.

THE SOUND FROM the television room was loud. What was Jake doing in there? He hadn't come out in three hours. Lauren had the day off, but she'd come back early and hadn't disturbed him. Now, she was getting worried. Going to the door, she listened for a moment. All she could hear was the booming sound of the television.

Slowly she opened the door, peering inside as if there was something she shouldn't see. The huge television screen was covered by war tanks, advancing toward an unknown enemy. Jake sat on the sofa, his posture erect as the action on the screen played out before him. He seemed mesmerized by the program.

"Jake," she called out to him. He didn't move, didn't look her way or react to her presence. She called out to him again, receiving the same nonreaction. Walking to the sofa, Lauren noticed the remote control next to Jake. Reaching over the back of the sofa, she picked it up and clicked the off button.

Jake whipped around.

"What are you doing?" she asked.

He said nothing for a long moment.

"I was watching a movie."

"You weren't. The movie was watching you. You were staring at that screen as if it had control of you."

"I was not."

Lauren came around the sofa and took a seat in front of Jake.

"This is me, Jake. You can talk to me. Why are you watching this movie?"

"I wanted to see something, test something," he said.

"The explosion," Lauren answered for him. "You want to see if the TV explosion and your explosion produce the same emotional results in you?"

"How did you know?"

"I was holding your hand in the theater when the explosion happened on-screen. Are you trying to recreate the feelings you had during the explosion that paralyzed your arm?"

"I'm trying to deal with it."

"Is this the best way? What would a psychologist or psychiatrist advise you to do?" Lauren asked. She wasn't sure if his watching movies was a good idea.

"I haven't consulted one."

His tone told her he had no plans to do so.

"All right. I'll watch with you." She turned the television back on and slipped into the seat next to him. "I need you to tell me what you're feeling."

She hit the back button to a part long before the explosion would take place. Jake was tense next to her. She sat close. While they weren't touching, she could feel his body heat and stay alert to changes in his demeanor.

"What is this about?" she asked.

"It's a war story, set in World War II. The

goal of the mission is to blow up a bridge to keep the enemy from being able to cross it."

Lauren recognized the story. It was an old black-and-white movie, for which she was silently thankful. Watching the explosion would be hard enough for him without the realistic blood and gore and special effects of more modern films. As they got closer to the scene, she took his hand. He was no longer glued to the screen, but there was a tenseness in his arm.

As the bomb exploded and soldiers were flung and killed, Lauren was the one to jump. She jerked his arm with the movement.

"Sorry," she said. For the rest of the movie, they remained silent. The Allies won and the world was set right.

"How do you feel?" she asked as the credits rolled.

"I'm wondering how you feel," he said. "The explosion seemed to affect you more than it did me."

"It's that huge screen. Even in black and white it was way too realistic."

"I'm fine," he said. "I felt none of the emotions that occurred that day."

"Pardon me for disagreeing with you, but that's not true. So tell me."

"Before you came in, I thought the explosion would force me to relive the incident, but it didn't."

Lauren didn't believe that it hadn't, not for a moment. She felt the way his arm tensed. She could see the way he held his body. The explosion had an effect on him, but he was a guy and a doctor, the worst kind of people to accept that something might be wrong with them.

"Are you planning to watch more of these?"

He shook his head. "I don't think I need to."

"I agree with that," she said.

"You're skeptical about the value of me watching them?"

"More like concerned," she said.

He smiled at her. "More than friends."

Lauren nodded. "Friends don't let friends watch explosions alone."

The mood lightened, but Lauren was unconvinced Jake hadn't been affected by the movie and she wanted to know now. Just as she was about to ask, he lifted his left hand and brushed a strand of her hair behind her ear. Waves of heat coursed from her face to her toes. She squeezed his hand harder and sought control.

Lauren fought to keep her plan in mind. Whenever he touched her or she touched him, all she could think of was how much she wanted to move closer to him.

"Tell me how you felt watching the explosion."

Jake shifted. "I don't suppose I can get you to drop this subject."

"I could, but you need to understand your response more than I do."

He thought about that for a moment, then spoke. "In the movie theater, the explosion was a surprise, just as it was in reality. Both times, it was the last thing I ever expected to happen. I tensed."

"Go on."

"For a moment, I relived the impact. I felt my body lifted from the ground and slammed against the building. I felt my arm bend under the pressure of my weight. Yet none of that happened in the theater, obviously. It was only in my mind."

"And today? Watching the explosions here?"

"These were different. I was ready for

them. I expected them to happen, and they didn't affect me. I didn't forget the impact or the feelings that came with my own experience, but I didn't feel them as I watched."

"Wonderful." She smiled.

"You know I do this just for you."

"What does that mean?"

"You're always so happy when I conquer something that I have told myself I can't do and you force me to try, anyway."

"Trying is what's important. You'll never succeed at anything if you don't try it first. I like it that you've been trying so hard."

"Thank you, teacher."

"Indeed," she said. "I'll get a chalk board and a ruler to drive the point home."

Jake laughed. "Don't. I can imagine you at the front of the classroom already."

He pulled her close, twisted his finger around loose strands of her hair. Lauren closed her eyes and stopped breathing.

"The next time you decide to watch a movie, invite me," she told him.

"What about Naliani? Suppose I choose a movie about a mother who loses a child."

Lauren visibly stiffened.

CHAPTER TWELVE

NO ONE KNEW better than Jake that we all have baggage we bring to every friendship or relationship. He certainly had his load to carry and Lauren had helped him lift it. As for him helping Lauren lift hers—he wished he could do something. But the one thing she had not done was forgive herself for the death of her daughter.

She hid it well. There was a glass shell around her that kept people out and held all her grief in. Just like those costumes she had worn, they made her someone else, even if just for a short while, someone who didn't have to face the realities of the world.

They were a pair, Jake thought. He'd been like that, unable to see that a change might be necessary. Then Lauren had come into his life like a godsend. He couldn't have ordered anyone better. She was both like him and different. She was starting over, but mostly by running away. He'd retreated into this apartment, while she planned to leave the city and go someplace new. The surroundings might help initially, but they wouldn't displace the grief. It would go with her.

"Why did you name her Naliani?" Jake asked.

Lauren gave him a watery smile. "She was conceived while we were on a business vacation in Indonesia. It's a surname there, but I loved it and we decided on it when she was born."

"I like it," he said. "Tell me about her."

Lauren shifted in her seat, drawing her knee under her. "She was the most beautiful child in the world."

"I had no doubt."

"She was smart and happy. She liked to dance around whenever she heard music playing. There was one commercial that had a lot of drums as a background. She'd hear it and immediately start to dance."

She smiled, but Jake saw her eyes begin to fill with water. She might cry, but she needed to revisit her daughter as much as he needed to revisit the explosion.

"Tell about the day she got sick?" He expected a kneejerk reaction from Lauren and he got one. She'd shifted on the couch. Moving closer to her, he put his arm around her shoulders. "Tell me," he whispered.

"She was fine when she went to bed that night. I read her a story. Her favorite book was about a dinosaur. Usually, she stayed awake until I finished reading, but that night she fell asleep. Still she felt perfectly well when I kissed her good-night."

Lauren paused. Jake was sure she was coming to the terror a mother must feel when she realized something was seriously wrong.

"I woke up hearing her crying. She was holding her head. Tears ran down her face and she was hot. Her temperature was too high to get her to the hospital without aid. I wrapped her in a blanket soaked in tepid water while Richard called for an ambulance."

Again, she paused. She took several long breaths as if she were drinking the air. Jake felt helpless. He wanted to do something, but there was nothing he could do, nothing he could say. It was a process and she had to go through it.

"We got her to the hospital." She stopped.

"You don't have to go on," Jake told her. "You're obviously in distress."

She nodded against him, her head on his shoulder. She dragged the air in and out, her mouth open. Jake patted her back, rubbed his hand up and down, trying to calm her. He should never have asked about her daughter. It was too painful a subject.

"They rushed everything, all the tests," she continued. "Because of how much pain she was in."

Her voice came out in short staccato bursts.

"It wasn't enough. By morning she was gone."

The last was delivered calmly as if all the weight she carried had fallen away. Jake was smart enough to know that only part of it was gone. But the healing process she needed had begun. He didn't push her off his shoulder. She stayed there until she fell asleep. He was comfortable holding her and she trusted him enough to open up to him. He would never forget that.

He felt useful, not useless. He'd helped

her. A surge of pride went through him. The closest he could get to how it felt was when he saved a patient's life for the first time. He was exhausted at the end of the ordeal, but the adrenaline flowing through his body could light up a small city.

He wasn't exhausted holding Lauren. He was falling in love with her and that alone gave him a powerful rush.

CAL HAD CALLED weekly since he'd been gone. There wasn't a routine. He didn't always call on the same day at the same time, but he checked in regularly. Jake didn't do the same and he was beginning to feel a little guilty about the one-way communication.

He picked up his phone and searched for his brother in the contacts list, then clicked on his number. Cal answered on the first ring.

"Jake, are you okay?"

His voice held concern. Jake could hear noise in the background, heavy trucks, men shouting.

"I'm fine," he said. "I thought I'd give you a call for a change."

Silence. Jake could almost see his brother's shoulders slump in relief.

"I'm glad you called."

"I won't keep you long. I can hear you're on a site."

"Don't bother about that," Cal said.

The noisy background suddenly quieted. Jake pictured Cal stepping into a construction trailer.

"Tell me what's going on," Cal said.

"Not much. I am driving now. I've been taking the car out several times a week."

"You've been doing what?" Cal asked, his voice rising.

"You heard me. I've been driving my car and I'm doing some consulting with the hospital."

Jake listened to the silence on the other end of the phone. He wasn't sure what Cal was thinking. He wanted him to be happy for him. He knew Cal was concerned about him, but he hadn't been here for the last three months. Lauren was here and Jake knew she was the reason for his progress, for the change in how he felt about himself.

"Are you sure that's a good idea?"

Jake heard the caution in his brother's voice.

"It's an excellent idea. And don't worry, I'm a lot more conservative than I used to be." Jake knew Cal was probably thinking of his wild days, his racing and participating in extreme sports. "Lauren is always in the car with me and I wouldn't take a risk and possibly hurt her."

"Do I hear a note of—"

"You do not." Jake was quick to erase that thought. There was nothing going on between them. Despite their kiss and some feelings he didn't want to take out of the box he'd stored them in, he didn't want to have Cal thinking a romance was going on.

"She's a beautiful woman. Most men would—"

"I'm not most men," he cut his brother off.

"I doubt she'd be concerned about your arm."

He knew she wouldn't. "Drop it, Cal. There's nothing going on there. What about you? Is there some female engineer you've discovered for more than her brain?"

Cal laughed. "Not yet, but I still look."

He implied Jake didn't. Since his fiancée had left him, Jake hadn't thought of women, but with Lauren in the apartment it was hard not to think of her.

"I have to go," Jake said. He wanted to end the call. It was getting too close to a subject he didn't want to pursue. "I have a consult with the hospital."

"At this hour?"

Jake checked the clock. It was ten o'clock in the evening. "You know doctors have crazy hours."

The brothers hung up and Jake thought about how much their relationship had improved. He wondered about himself after the accident and how he'd treated those around him. If Cal hadn't hired Lauren, would Jake still be sitting in a silent apartment watching the sun rise and set and doing nothing in between?

LAUREN GROANED, BUT REFUSED to open her eyes. She didn't know what time it was and didn't want to know. The night had been long, first with her telling Jake the full details of Naliani's death and then falling asleep on him. She woke up on the sofa with a blanket over her for the second time. Then she went to bed.

Even though she was tired, she felt as if something calm had settled inside her. Maybe telling Jake the story had helped her in some way. She encouraged her patients to tell her everything about their ailments and even things about their lives. She was an advocate for healing the whole body.

Until now, it had never been her body.

And speaking of body, it was time to get up. Pushing the covers back, she swung her legs to the floor and lay there, half in and half out of the bed. It wasn't normal for her to stay in bed so long. As an intern, she'd become accustomed to jumping out of the covers, instantly awake and ready to go. In her practice, she was often in the office before most of the staff arrived. Amy being the exception.

Since giving up her practice and staying in this apartment, she'd established a routine, but it had room for an occasional lapse.

A shower refreshed her. She was light-footed and humming a happy tune when she went down the stairs to the main room.

"Good morning," Jake said as she stepped off the last rung. "How do you feel?"

"Isn't that the question I should be asking

you?" Lauren didn't want to tell him how she felt. She was better now, although when she woke, last night was as clear in her mind as when she was lying against him on the sofa in the media room.

"I'm wonderful," he said. "And since I am not the patient this morning..."

"Patient?" She latched onto the word.

"Bad choice of words," he said. "Since I am not in pain or in need of assistance, I thought we should do something that's all about you."

"Me?"

He nodded. "You've previously taken me on drives, picnics and parties, all to show me something, teach me something or have me observe something. Because of your hard work, you deserve a reward. What would you like to do?"

"I get it," Lauren said. "Because of me crying on your shoulder last night, you are going to show me something, teach me something or have me observe something and I get to choose what it is."

"Don't take all the fun out of it. This gesture comes from my heart."

He made an exaggerated bow, putting his hand over his heart. Lauren smiled.

"All right," she said. There was so much going on in New York all the time. Where could they go that she hadn't been and wouldn't see anyone who knew her? "The Circle Line Tour."

"A ferry tour, with the tourists?" Jake asked.

Lauren knew she was unlikely to run into anyone she knew there. Even her former patients who lived in New York rarely went to any of the attractions that thousands of tourists flocked to see. And she did want to see some of the sights of the city. While she'd lived in Brooklyn, her schedule rarely left her time for a day to herself. She was either reading medical information, attending seminars, seeing patients or worrying about their symptoms. When Naliani came along, her time was more precious and harder to schedule than before.

"The tourists won't eat you." She smiled. "You've been on this tour before, right?"

"Not since I was twelve."

"Good, then you won't remember anything they told you because at twelve you weren't listening. You were too busy either being an attention-getting jerk or trying to get noticed by a girl who wasn't giving you the time of day."

Jake laughed. "So true, so true. You go put on your sailor coat and I'll check the dock times."

Lauren's heart lifted. She was wearing long pants and a shirt, but on the water she'd need a jacket and possibly a hat. Definitely sunglasses. She ran up the stairs. She didn't have sailing clothes, but she knew the ferry was a little old and utilitarian. Anyone dressed to the nines would stand out like a polar bear in the Sahara.

The taxi ride was short as they got out on Pier 83. Jake must have gotten the tickets online, since they went right to the lineup to board.

"What time do we get on?" she asked.

"It leaves at ten, so a few minutes before that I suppose. Afterward, we'll have lunch."

The ship sailed right on schedule. Lauren was pleased with the upgraded amenities Jake had added. She sat in her plush chair and watched as the city unfolded before them. The guide gave information she'd never heard before. She had known that the superrich of the early nineteenth century had vast homes that were either apartment buildings now or had been completely demolished and something else stood in their place.

Jake watched her more than he looked at the skyline.

"You're staring at me," she said when they went under the second bridge.

"You're fascinating," he told her.

"How?"

"I never know what you're going to say next, even right now." He shrugged. "Your eyes are as big as saucers. You're looking at everything as if you've never seen it before."

"I haven't," she said. "This is a whole new world."

He smiled, but said nothing.

The cruise lasted two and half hours. When Lauren stepped back on the pier, her knees gave way for a second or two. Being back on land took some getting used to. Jake was there holding her arm. He seemed a lot more comfortable with his arm, accepting it as part of him instead of trying to hide it.

Their lobster lunch had them laughing

at some of the sights they'd seen and the anecdotes the guide had used. Lauren was having fun. It had been a long time since anyone put her first. She was the receiver, not the caregiver that afternoon. Lauren liked being with Jake. He was charming and funny when he wanted to be. She also knew he put on a mask to hide his true feelings from the world. It was normal. Everyone had some sort of defense mechanism. Hadn't he told her she hid behind a glass wall and wouldn't let anyone in?

He was wrong about that. He'd found the crack in the glass and slipped through it before she had a chance to seal it closed.

"More coffee?" a waiter asked.

Lauren hadn't noticed him arrive. She shook her head, placing a palm over her coffee cup. "I'm good."

Jake shook his head too. They each still had half a cup.

"What else would you like to do today?" Jake asked, taking a sip of his coffee.

Lauren thought a moment, biting her bottom lip.

"It's your day," he said.

"I want to go for a ride in a hansom carriage."

"You're kidding," he said.

Smiling, she shook her head.

"You're quite the tourist."

"Come on," she laughed. "You know you want to do it too, but the tough guy in you is scared people will find out." She stared directly at him, lowering her eyes. "Don't worry, I'm the keeper of secrets."

"HANSOM CARRIAGES ARE such a part of New York that most people believe they started here," the driver said.

Lauren and Jake were seated behind the driver as he began his trek through Central Park.

"In truth," he continued, "they were developed in England and didn't come here for a long time."

Lauren turned to Jake. "See, the stuff you learn when you act like a tourist."

He smiled and settled back against the seat. "I admit it has been a learning experience. Without you, I never would have done this."

"You don't like it?" She leaned forward, looking at him from the side.

"I didn't mean that. I am enjoying myself. I just never expected to."

"You mean when you went on those trips as a doctor, you never wandered around the cities and took in the sites?"

"Some," he said.

But Lauren had the feeling the some he visited were likely none.

"Why haven't you already visited these places?" he asked.

"I have seen some of them. I've been to the Met, Columbus Circle, top of the Empire State Building, Statue of Liberty—"

"All right, you can stop. So you aren't the typical New Yorker."

"I'm from Maryland, but the place doesn't matter. There are people who like to see things they've only read about and people who find just knowing about them is okay."

"People can change," Jake said.

"Yes," she agreed.

"I enjoyed the history and the little bits of information that books don't tell you. I might be interested in visiting more places."

"What about when you go back to work?" she asked. "Are you going to be so driven that you never have time for anything except medicine from then on?"

He smiled and looked away a moment. "I notice you said *when* I go back to work."

"Of course you're going back. You love medicine and you love working."

"I agree, medicine is a demanding mistress and I have missed her during these last two years, but I don't want to go back to the schedule I had."

"Why is that?"

"Someone opened my eyes to the fact that there are things outside of medicine."

"But you're known for doing all kinds of things in your old life. You did stuff that had nothing to do with medicine."

"I *did*," he corrected. "After I started surgery, there was no more time. I had to keep up with new techniques, innovations in the field, new procedures."

"Every doctor has to do that."

"I made it my life," he said.

"I don't think you can help that. It's hard to go on a vacation while there is someone suffering."

"I guess we understand each other," Jake said.

The carriage took them much deeper into the park than the paths they had walked and far away from the apartment building. They got down from the hansom cat and Jake used his left hand to pull her arm through his right one. They walked that way for several blocks.

"Is there anything else you'd like to do? There's still plenty of daylight left or we could go home, change and go out again."

"There's one other place I'd like to go today," she told him.

"Your wish, if possible," he cautioned, "is my command."

Lauren didn't join in his playfulness. "It's in Brooklyn."

"Then we'll need a car."

Lauren drove. Jake was extremely competent behind the wheel, but she knew where they were going. Jake seemed to have tapped into her mood. He rode without asking questions about their destination. He didn't give her any inquiring looks or frowns. When she drove through the gates of the cemetery, he only glanced in her direction.

"How often have you come here?" Jake asked as they got out of the car. He took her arm as if she needed support.

"Not for several months. I used to come

every day. Amy made me understand that wasn't healthy. If we hadn't talked last night, I'm not sure I would have come today."

She squeezed his arm in thanks.

It's beautiful," Jake said as they stood in front of Naliani's gravestone.

It was a child angel, its wings unfurled, its face as innocent as that of a newborn.

"Richard chose it," she said.

Jake put his arm around her and pulled her into his side. "Do you want to be alone?" he asked gently.

She shook her head. "I've always been alone here. Thank you for being with me."

They didn't stay long. And tears didn't fill Lauren's eyes or slide down her cheeks. She wasn't here to say goodbye. She loved her daughter and always would. She was here for peace, to see if that calmness that she'd felt when she woke would be different as she stood in front of her child's grave. She didn't break. She felt different, some emotion she didn't understand, but she knew she could go on, that she could continue seeing children as patients and not have the experience break her.

She stepped back, indicating she was

done. Jake didn't relinquish his hold, but walked her back to the car in his careful embrace. This time he drove back to the apartment.

"Hungry?" he asked as they went inside.

They hadn't eaten since they got off the cruise and that was hours ago now. Jake went to the kitchen.

"I'm not hungry," Lauren called behind him.

He came back carrying a tray in one hand. On it was a bottle of wine, already open, glasses, a plate of fresh fruit, some cheese and bread.

"I didn't do this," he answered her questioning glance. "Except for the wine, everything was already set up."

"Put the tray down," she said, glancing at a table in front of the sofa.

Jake did as instructed and turned back to her.

"Thank you," she said.

"For today?"

She nodded. "For understanding. For thinking of me. For listening to me cry and not judging me." She paused and took a step toward him. They were only a couple of feet apart. Shifting even closer, she held his right hand. "I realized this morning that I was also missing something. I was virtually unable to use my heart, my emotions because I'd let my entire being be eclipsed by the loss of Naliani.

"I gave up my home, my colleagues, my friends, my job. I thought that moving away and beginning again would solve my problem, make it less painful. But it wouldn't. I was afraid. I should have gone immediately, but I met Caleb and he gave me an opportunity to stay. Then I met you and you did the same, although you challenged me to the brink. There were times when I wanted to throw my hands up and walk out. But the thought of being out there alone was more frightening than staying here."

"I'm sorry I treated you so badly."

She smiled and Jake did too.

"It's all right. It helped in the long run. Then last night happened. It felt like a sort of breakthrough. I'm not sure what it meant, but I knew when I woke this morning that everything was going to be all right."

She rested her cheek on his chest.

"So thank you for giving me the use of my arm back."

Jake didn't say anything. She felt his heart beat faster. His hand reached under her chin and pulled her face up to his. Tenderly his mouth met hers. Lauren melted against him.

She'd been falling for him and his kiss only told her that the crush she had on Jake years ago had not died, but been reborn.

CHAPTER THIRTEEN

EVERYTHING AROUND JAKE seemed to change after the night Lauren told him about her daughter. Their lives changed. They laughed more, danced a lot and spent hours each day outside. Sometimes they joined the throngs of tourists visiting one of New York's landmarks and other times they spent the day driving and talking with no apparent destination in mind.

They'd see a road sign and decide to find out where it led. Jake liked this new venture into the unknown. When Naliani's name was mentioned, there was no pain associated with it. The pain Jake had in his arm and shoulder all but disappeared. He let Lauren's magic hands massage him to make sure it didn't come back. And he liked her touch.

She chose romances or musicals for them to watch, and he chose action flicks. They enjoyed them all, but mainly he loved talking to her, hearing her laugh and watching her move about the apartment. She hummed a lot and he knew she was happier now than she'd been before.

Who would think so much between them could change for the better? Jake had compared her to his ex-girlfriend in the beginning, but the two were as different as night and day. Lauren was everything he could want in a woman. They hadn't shared another kiss since that night, but he couldn't forget how she felt in his arms. He wanted to make her happy. There were times when he'd drift off into thought about things he could do to make her smile.

Jake was falling in love and there was nothing he could do about it. He'd passed the point of wanting to do anything about it a long while ago.

THE KITCHEN IN Amy's brownstone smelled of baking bread and homemade pies.

"What is this?" Lauren asked as she came inside.

"I can't explain it," Amy said. "I thought I'd make a little dinner for us and somewhere between the sofa and the stove I lost my head. I kept going and going as if the army was coming by for cake and coffee."

"I guess I'll have to do. There's no way I can eat all this, but that bread smells delicious."

Soon they were sitting down to dinner and wine.

"I didn't know you could cook so well," Lauren said. "When we worked together, occasionally you'd bring in food, but nothing like this."

"Anyone can cook. It just takes a little getting used to your equipment." She gestured toward the oven. "And reading the directions."

"I never had time for that. I was too busy suturing someone's cut."

"Maybe it's something else you and Jake can do together. From what you've told me, if he can drive a car, he can use a measuring cup."

Lauren laughed. She had a mental picture of Jake with flour all over him. Then the picture changed to her cleaning the flour off of him.

"Have you told him yet who you are?"

Lauren shook her head. "I know I should.

He's asked me to stay until his brother gets back. I don't know when that is, but it has to be later than when the school year would begin. He knows I don't have a job I'm going to, so I can stay as long as I choose."

"You like him, don't you?" Amy raised her glass of wine, but she didn't take her eyes off Lauren.

"Don't be silly."

"I'm not being silly. I'm being your friend. I can tell when someone changes and you have a glow about you. That glow that goes with falling in love."

"I'm not in love," she denied.

"Maybe not yet, but you're on your way. Otherwise, telling him you're a doctor wouldn't mean anything to you. If he fired you, it would mean nothing, but you want to stay. If he hadn't asked you to stay, you'd have done so anyway."

"I wouldn't. I have been looking for property and a job."

"Where?" Amy's eyebrows went up. "This is the first I'm hearing of this."

"In Arizona. I thought the Southwest would be a good place to settle."

"Arizona? Do you know anyone in Arizona?"

"No, and isn't that the point? Starting over means leaving everything behind."

"Everything and everyone?" Amy asked.

"Not you," Lauren stated. "But I need a fresh beginning."

"What about Jake? Isn't he a fresh beginning?"

"That's not what I mean and you know it."

"Yes," Amy said. "I know what you mean, but you've been at that apartment for nearly three months and it's obvious you have feelings for the man that go beyond medical care." She paused. Lauren didn't say anything. "He could be the beginning you're looking for."

"I won't deny that I like Jake a lot. But he's not ready for a relationship. He's got so much anger and doubt on his plate that it's hard for him to see through it."

"Maybe you should make him open his eyes wider with your next project."

IT DIDN'T LOOK like there would be another project. Lauren checked her mailbox on her way back from Amy's and, as if broaching the subject made it come true, there was a letter waiting for her from Kingman, Arizona.

The map of the United States covered the computer screen in Lauren's room. She looked at the distance between New York and Arizona. It was only the span of her hand on the monitor, but in reality she was looking at thousands of miles, a different climate, different seasonal expectations. The foliage would be new to her and there were coyotes roaming the streets.

Wasn't all that change what she was looking for? So why was she hesitating? There was a medical practice she could join until she was comfortable enough to strike out on her own again. She'd be a world away from her father, who lived in Maine, and her sisters, who lived in Maryland. Both had suggested she come and stay near them, but Lauren didn't think that was far enough from the memories that New York held.

Should she accept the position? How long would they hold it for her? There had to be other candidates.

Lauren closed the computer screen. She'd talk to Jake about it. He knew she was planning to leave. He'd asked her to stay, but when opportunity presented itself, she needed to decide if she wanted to take it or not.

Why shouldn't she go? she asked herself. If she had a checklist, she could tick off everything she'd required in this offer. Had she become too close to Jake? He needed her; she knew that even if he didn't. If she moved on, he'd have to start over with someone else and Lauren could only imagine the type of personality needed to deal with Jake. He'd retreat into his anger.

But was that a reason for her to alter her plans? Lauren took a long time to ponder that. He was still a man suffering and she had become someone he could talk to. In her capacity as a doctor, what should she do? Was she responsible for his well being, for his attitude, for what his reaction would be without her? It was unfair of her to think that she was the only person able to cope with his mood changes or the only one who could get him to fight for life and not sit in his apartment all day.

Getting up, she wondered where Jake was. She couldn't put this off. Lauren had no answer. She was torn between Jake's needs and her own. The only resolution was to talk to him. She'd do it now.

He was sitting on the sofa amid the tall windows reading a book. Lauren walked down the stairs with determination. She went directly to where he sat and took the chair opposite him. He lowered the book to his lap.

"You've been up there a long time," he said.

"I have a job offer." She blurted the words out before she could stop herself.

"Where?"

He leaned back against the cushions. Lauren could see the stiffness in his body.

"Arizona?"

"Do you know anyone in Arizona?"

It was the same question Amy had asked. Lauren shook her head.

"Why did you decide to apply there?"

"You know I wanted a new beginning. It seemed like a good place. Everything about it would be far different from this side of the country."

The atmosphere in the room had turned

serious. The sun was up, but Lauren felt as if twilight had fallen.

"Are you going to accept?" Jake asked.

Lauren thought she heard him holding his breath. Maybe she wanted to think that.

"I haven't decided. I wanted to talk to you about it."

"It's not my decision," he said. "You told me straight out when you came that you were on your way somewhere else. I knew sooner or later you would have to deal with that decision."

"Do you want me to go?" she asked.

Jake looked away, then back. "That's an unfair question. I asked you to stay until Cal returned, but you're not obligated to do that. If you have a place you want to go, then you have to decide."

Want. Lauren latched onto the word. Did she *want* to go to Arizona? She could be a doctor anywhere. As far as Jake knew, she could be a kindergarten teacher anywhere. She'd been to Arizona once for a medical conference. It was in Phoenix, but this job would be in the small town of Kingman near both the tip of Nevada and the California border.

"Arizona seems a long way for a school system to hire a kindergarten teacher. Don't they have enough teachers out there?"

"I don't know," Lauren said honestly, but Jake had found a hole in her story that she had not thought through. "Maybe I was the best candidate."

"For kindergarten?"

"Well, I told them I was planning to move," she said.

Jake cocked his head to the side as if he was weighing the information.

"How long do you have to make the decision?"

"They didn't say in the offer, but I'm sure I'll have to give them an answer within a week. School starts the beginning of September."

There was no calendar in the room, but mentally they both knew October was only a few weeks away.

Lauren stood up and walked to one of the large windows. She looked out over New York. She'd grown up in Maryland, gone to medical school in DC and lived in New York City since graduating. She loved the beat of the city. It was huge and there was a lot to do. If she moved to Kingman, the entire population was less than thirty thousand. It would be what she told herself she wanted. Somehow a new beginning no longer held the appeal it once did.

Did that have something to do with Jake? Was Amy right? Did she really want Jake to ask her to stay?

Speaking of Jake, he came over and stood next to her. "What are you thinking?" he asked.

"I was comparing New York to Kingman."

"And?" he asked.

Again she thought he was holding his breath.

Lauren hung her head. "And I haven't decided. But I will. And I'll let you know."

She reached up and ran her hand down his arm several times.

"I'll miss you," he said, as if he was sure her decision was to leave.

JAKE WAS ABOUT to lose Lauren. She'd made her decision. There wasn't anything more to say. She'd told him the day they met that her time was short. So now that she was planning to put that into action, it shouldn't come as a surprise to him.

He turned back and stared at her.

"You know, you never call her LeeLee," Jake said.

"What?"

"You said you called your daughter LeeLee, yet you always refer to her by her given name."

Lauren looked away. For a long moment nothing happened. Jake didn't think she was going to explain. Then she looked back at him.

"This is going to sound weird."

Her voice was barely a whisper. He had to strain to hear her.

"After she was gone, it's like there was no LeeLee. Whenever I hear it, my mind hears the way LeeLee said it. The high-pitched sound of her five-year-old voice, with her tongue between her teeth. The pain is more intense when I think of the name in her voice."

"It doesn't sound so weird," Jake told her.

Lauren looked as if she was relieved.

"What about other children?"

"Other children?" she frowned.

"You're a young, beautiful woman. I assumed you'd want a family?"

Lauren swallowed and Jake thought he might be getting too personal.

"I did," she said quietly, almost reverently. "I haven't thought about it for a long time."

"Now that you're starting over, you can add it back to your to-do list."

She smiled. "You're funny, you know?"

"Why so?"

"Talking about having a baby as if it was something you put between 'pick up green beans' and 'have the television repaired.'"

"Isn't it?" he laughed.

The instant he saw the expression on Lauren's face, Jake regretted his words.

"I'm sorry," he apologized. "I didn't mean that. I was only joking."

"It's all right, Jake. You can't protect me from innocent comments and I don't want you to feel like you have to."

"I respect you so much," Jake said.

"Oh?"

"Through all that you have to contend with, you're still considerate of someone else's feelings."

"Isn't that what doctors do? I mean you

have a life too. Yet you still have to deal with the worry or heartbreak of another person, for instance."

"But you're not a doctor," he told her.

"But everyone has to accept life and move on. The world won't stop for either of us, regardless of what happens to us, or what we do for a living."

Lauren was quiet a moment. Jake knew he'd brought up memories that were painful, but she'd taught him to face his. She needed to do the same.

"You're right. We each have to face the day. And you running away won't change things either."

Her head whipped around and she stared at him. "I'm not running away."

"What do you call it?" Jake asked.

"Starting over. I'm going to a place that needs a…needs me and putting down roots."

"You're licking your wounds in hopes that they will heal. Running away gives you new surroundings, maybe new friends, but at night when the lights go out and there is nothing in the dark but you and your thoughts, the change of scenery won't mean anything."

Lauren dropped her eyes and looked at the floor.

"I know," Jake said softly. "It's how you found me."

"Physician, heal thyself," Lauren said almost too quietly for him to hear.

"Exactly," he agreed. "I wouldn't have done it, at least not immediately. If you hadn't come along, I don't know where I'd be right now, maybe still sitting in this room hiding from the world. But you did come along. I was your Naliani."

"You weren't." Her voice was strong in denial.

Jake nodded. "I represented the child you couldn't help. You saw in me all the symptoms that you missed in your daughter. And you weren't going to let me die, as it were. You pushed, cajoled, judged and guilt-tripped me to get up and live. *You* have to do the same."

"Leave me alone," Lauren shouted, getting up and leaving.

"Don't. Wait." Jake got up too. He stepped up to her and looked into her eyes.

"Face it, Lauren. You didn't miss the symptoms of meningitis. It struck fast. There was nothing you could have done. But you can't bury your heart with LeeLee." He deliberately used her daughter's nickname.

Lauren's eyes blazed like red-hot coals.

"You're still alive. I know your heart hurts. I know all the things you feel."

"You don't," she whispered. "You can't possibly know how I feel."

Jake shook his head. "You're right. I don't know what it feels like to lose a child, but I do know what it's like to die inside because of something you couldn't control." He paused to see her reaction.

Lauren stood like a pillar, as unforgiving as a rock.

"Is this how you're going to live your life? Locked away from the world, helping others, but never allowing anyone to get close to you?"

"I don't do that."

Jake wasn't about to give up. She meant too much to him, and he knew this meant too much to her. Her whole future was at stake. Lauren stepped back. He reached for her hand, held it firmly.

"Since your divorce, how many dates have you been on?"

"What does that have to do with anything?" Lauren questioned.

Jake didn't want to argue with her, but he promised himself he'd see this through. "What it means is you'd be letting go. While your grief hasn't left you and it never will, you're still among the living. So, you should *live*. Do all the things you're supposed to do, and that includes being open to others. Stop walking around closed off to what people can offer you. You deserve everything."

"Who are you?" she asked with a bitterness in her voice that he'd never heard before. "Have you been sitting around all day thinking all this up, and now you want to analyze me?"

Jake let that go. He knew the question came from anger. "It's not me analyzing you, Lauren. You're angry."

"You're right, I am."

She tried to move past him, but he reached for her hand again.

"It's not me you're angry with. It's the truth."

Her brows rose. "I'm angry with the truth?"

He nodded. "You can tell yourself anything you want, but I've hit a button you didn't want pressed and you're upset because you know I'm right. You're the one who's taken on the role of caregiver, yet you need as much care as I did."

"Please let me go." Lauren's tone was laced with venom.

"Going to your room won't change anything. Just like leaving the city and starting somewhere else won't absolve you of the guilt you feel. All the feelings you have are in here and in here." He pointed to her head and then to her heart. "They follow you, invisible, yet are always there, weighing you down. Until you deal them, you'll never be alive."

"Jake, move aside." Each word was spoken succinctly like a warning bell.

Jake let her hand drop. He crossed the room and made a grand gesture with his free arm, indicating the open space to Lauren.

She took a deep breath and passed him. She didn't run out of the room, but when she reached the steps, she rushed up them as if fire burned her feet.

LAUREN'S CHEST HEAVED as she closed the door to her bedroom. She hated Jake for what he'd said about her. It wasn't true. She *was* moving on. She was changing states, changing almost everything about herself. She no longer had to pull herself out of bed in the morning or force herself to go through mundane things like washing her face and brushing her teeth. She'd resumed eating regularly and gained back some of the weight she'd lost. She would still be a children's doctor.

So why was she feeling as if she couldn't breathe? Jake had said some harsh things that she didn't want to hear. She denied some of it, but she knew part of it was true. Had he been right? Was she really angry because what she was really doing was refusing to go on? Lauren hadn't had a date since her divorce. She'd had men show an interest in her. It was hard not to know when someone found her attractive. Even Jake had looked at her that way on occasion. And except for him, she'd refused all comers.

She told herself that she'd lost everything, her child, her marriage, and those were the reasons she wasn't ready to start another serious relationship. But she knew enough time had passed where she should be ready to meet men. She'd used her practice as a shield to keep from doing that, telling herself and Amy that she was too busy. At the end of the day, she was too tired to do anything but sleep. And told herself that she would get around to dating sooner or later. In her mind, it was always later.

Then, thanks to that ad, she'd realized Jake was in town, and now, she didn't know if that was a trigger telling her to try to move on with her life, or not. She just knew she wanted to see him. Maybe, in the back of her mind, she thought reconnecting with him could reconnect her with an innocent time in her life, before her marriage, her child's birth and subsequent death.

And where had that led her?

Here, hiding in her bedroom, angry with the man who'd forced her to see herself in a true mirror. Not one that reflected the beautiful life of the princess after the prince finds her and they go on to their happily-ever-after. But one that showed her naked with scars, one that reflected who she was in stark sunlight and not clouded by fairy-tales or rose-colored glasses.

There was some truth to what he said. She

hadn't thought about it before, and she denied it to Jake, but she had been using him as her LeeLee. She was trying to save him. She'd pushed, forced him to confront things in his life, when her life was just as messy.

She couldn't save LeeLee. But what about Jake? She knew the signs with him. She could see his symptoms and act on them before it was too late.

Was there anything wrong in that?

Wouldn't she have done the same for her daughter if she could have? Shouldn't she try to make Jake see that even if she had been treating him as if he were LeeLee, her pushing and prodding him were working?

She opened the door and went back downstairs. Jake stood in the same place she'd left him. He said nothing when he saw her. It was her turn to open the conversation.

"I'm sorry," she began. "I did think of you in terms of my daughter. I tried to see in you what I missed in her, just like you said. But it's not necessarily a bad thing if it's helped you rejoin the living."

He took a step forward. Lauren held up a hand.

"I still intend to move away. This is not

the place for me. Even if I know my baggage goes with me, I believe it will be easier to deal with if I'm not surrounded on a day-to-day basis with reminders of her and how I missed seeing her symptoms."

"Lauren, that's not true. That type of disease strikes quickly. Even if you had thought something was wrong, there's no guarantee you could have done anything more or anything different than you did."

"That may be true and I'll have to come to terms with it."

"But those terms will be somewhere out of New York."

She nodded.

"All right, but make me a promise."

Lauren stiffened. "What is it?"

"Give yourself a time limit, say one year. If your life is no better in the new place, you will return to the city and deal with it here."

"Why?"

"Because here is where it happened. Here is your home. And here is where you will heal."

Lauren felt as if their roles had been reversed. He was the doctor, diagnosing her and suggesting treatment. Like any of her patients, she needed to take her own medicine.

"I agree," she told him.

IT HAD BEEN two long days and nights and Lauren had not made her decision to go or stay. Jake was on a consulting call on the third day. She didn't disturb him when he was talking to other doctors. She considered it therapy for him.

Getting a cup of coffee, she went to the media room. If the loud explosions helped Jake with his trauma, maybe a movie about a child could help her. Jake had thrown the suggestion out. At the time he wasn't really telling her to do it, but Lauren recognized that she had a heavy burden to carry and she needed to see if she could lighten the weight.

She didn't know if Jake's vast library of DVDs had anything to suit her needs, but she'd check.

Before she had a chance to look for movies, she noticed a book lying on the coffee table. This time it wasn't a yearbook. This one was small. It looked worn, as if it had been read many times. The pages were yellowed and the cover had a photo of a little blond child on it. Lauren recognized the look of a Down syndrome baby even before she read the cover.

She knew of the book, *Angel Unaware*, by the 1950s film star Dale Evans. A few of Lauren's patients had Down syndrome and at least two parents had mentioned how that book had comforted and inspired them. She'd never read it, but on occasion had recommended it to distressed moms and dads.

She wondered why it was here. Had Jake left it for her? He was a surgeon, who specialized in orthopedics. Why would he have such a well-read book about a Down syndrome child? She opened the book to the first page and started to read. Within seconds she was fully engaged. Taking a seat, she read on, never relaxing, but sitting on the edge of the sofa as she listened to Robin, a two-and-a-half-year-old, tell her story with its deeply moving message about her passing.

Lauren was in tears when she closed the cover. It was a short book, less than a hundred pages, but it was uplifting. She hoped Naliani had met Robin and that the two of them were together. Lauren understood now that Naliani was a gift, that her child had been put on this earth to enrich her life, and the lives of everyone she'd met, and if Lauren moved away, ran away as Jake had suggested, she'd not only be letting down the those she could help, but she'd let Naliani down too.

A weight lifted from her shoulders. Her decision was made. She called the Kingman Clinic and informed them that she would not be joining their staff.

She no longer needed to watch a movie.

She needed to tell Jake, but not just yet. She had to do something else first.

CHAPTER FOURTEEN

WITH THE BOOK in her hand, Lauren left the apartment. She had to go and see Naliani. It took longer to reach the cemetery by subway, but she made it there. The angel stood above the grave as though welcoming Lauren. It was the first time, she'd ever felt that way. As before, no tears misted her eyes, yet her heart was heavy for her daughter, for the future they wouldn't have together and the life Naliani wouldn't have.

The book in her hand told of another mother who resolved the loss of her child by focusing on the time they had together instead of the time lost. Lauren sat on a bench and looked at the inscribed name and dates associated with her daughter. She looked at the small dash separating her birth and death years.

"What did you give me?" she asked. "Unconditional love. The joys of motherhood.

The laughter we shared. The miracle of seeing you grow before my eyes, of you teaching me to see all the wonder of the world around us."

Lauren spoke the words aloud, quietly saying them as if praying. Lauren hoped that in some sense her daughter could hear her, and understand that Jake was right. Lauren had to live, had to go on and know that she still had her daughter's love.

"I love you, LeeLee. I will always love you." A tear fell, but not a sad one. It was a happy tear for the time they had spent together. "You have a special place in my heart and it will be open forever."

Lauren looked again at the book in her hand and thanked Dale Evans and her daughter Robin. She walked down the path she'd taken earlier and emerged out onto the street. Taking a quick look back, she smiled. This time the angel seemed to smile. Lauren knew LeeLee was okay.

The world looked different when you made a major decision, she thought. Good or bad, it gave you a direction to follow. Lauren checked the sky. The sun shone brightly. The noise and passion of the streets of New York were back. She didn't think the crowds were too thick or the traffic too loud. She only thought about how much she loved this city.

SHE *WAS* LEAVING. She *wasn't* leaving. Jake felt like he was on a merry-go-round or a roller coaster. He'd go up and down, feeling elated with what Lauren said, then fall down as if the bottom dropped out of his world. How had he gotten to this place? He didn't want her to leave his apartment, much less New York. Eventually Cal would return and there would be no need for him to have a constant companion.

If she remained in the city, they could see each other, talk, even play tennis or take long rides in the country. She'd postponed her trip to help him in the beginning and he couldn't completely believe that her decision to remain would have nothing to do with him and his needs. Lauren was a caregiver. He'd run into them before in his profession. She was both compassionate and a straight shooter. She understood when someone needed a soft touch and when they needed a good kick in the butt. He'd been the recipient of each and he was all the better for it.

Although she was from Maryland, she seemed like such a New Yorker, like this was her piece of ground and she would defend it against all comers. Jake had lived here all his life and while he'd been to most of the world's capitals, he couldn't think of living anywhere else.

"How was your call?" Lauren asked, bringing Jake back to the present. He'd been so involved in his own thoughts that he'd almost forgotten she was sitting across from him.

He glanced at the computer screen, which could have been a foreign object. He felt like his call had been years ago.

"It was fine."

"Are you considering going into the hospital and talking face-to-face?"

"Even if I'm not, you are," he said.

Lauren smiled and Jake's heart flipped. How did she do that? "It won't hurt you. You're a lot less self-conscious about people staring at your arm, so is there a reason you don't want to go to the hospital?"

"Yeah, there are doctors there."

Lauren laughed. "You do remember, you're one of them?"

"They'll want to examine me, even though my test rests aren't in yet. They'll ask how I am."

"You can answer how you are and you can have an exam or refuse one. You're strong enough to assert your wishes and have them obeyed."

"Except with you."

And so the next morning after tennis Lauren drove him to the hospital. As he walked through the areas where he'd worked for years, the staff called out "glad to see you," or "welcome back" and "you're looking great," yet no one asked how he was or offered to check his arm. Jake was sure Lauren had put the word in someone's ear.

He was grateful for her. The woman had superpowers. He wouldn't be surprised if the next time he saw her, she was wearing a cape and mask. Then he laughed out loud. He'd imagined her in the costume, large dark eyes peeking out of the mask.

LAUREN DIDN'T HEAR him talking, but he was still in his office. She knocked lightly on the door and opened it when he called out to her.

Poking her head inside, she saw him sitting at his desk in front of his computer. He motioned her to come in. "I forgot to ask. Where'd you get to on your day off?"

"Oh, I had to talk to someone," Lauren said. His brows rose, but she didn't offer any other information. "Did you leave this book for me?" she asked, taking a seat and holding out the copy.

"I thought it might help."

"Have you read it?"

"A very long time ago," he said.

"It looked as if it had been read many times."

"It belonged to my grandmother," Jake said. "She had a special needs child who died. I didn't know that until she died and I was helping my mother go through her things. There was a photo of a child. His name and age were written on the back. Until you told me about Naliani, I'd forgotten about the picture and the book."

"LeeLee," she corrected and watched Jake's reaction. It was a slight smile. "Anyway, thank you. It did help. I've made a decision about Arizona." She addressed Jake directly. Did he stiffen? She wasn't sure.

"What is it?" he asked, spreading his hands.

I'm not going."

Jake slowly leaned forward in his chair. He took a long breath. "What changed your mind?"

"You did. You and Dale Evans."

"You're can't make this decision because of me."

Lauren laughed. "I can't totally rule you out, either, but my decision is not about you or the promise I made to stay until Caleb returns." She looked at the book in her hand. "I'm doing it for Naliani. And as you pointed out, my location doesn't matter. Whatever problems I've had would go with me. I can be happy here too. I might have to work at it a bit, not take things so seriously, but in time everything will work out. So, for now, you're stuck with me. I'll stay until Caleb gets back."

"I don't consider myself being stuck."

She smiled. "We are a pair," she said. "And since I'm not going to Arizona, I will have to decide where I am going when I leave here."

"You're still leaving the city?"

She shrugged. "Maybe. I've sold my house. I could start over here or maybe a suburb not too far away and get the best of both worlds. This is a very expensive city. Regardless, I'll need to look for a place to live and a full-time job. My sisters and father have asked me to settle near them. My dad lives in Maine and my sisters are in Maryland. I'd have family nearby in both of those places, but I'm not sure about that. And I've sort of rediscovered New York, thanks to you."

She couldn't read his mood. He looked like he wanted to argue with her and congratulate her, all at the same time.

"Any word on when Caleb will be returning?" she asked.

"You've just decided not to go to Arizona. Now you want to know the date you can leave here?" Jake asked.

"It would be good to know. I wouldn't want to find someplace to live and have to refuse it again."

"I don't know about Cal," he said. "When we talked, he didn't mention an end date."

Lauren nodded. She'd have to ask him the next time they talked.

THEY'D HAD ANOTHER incredible day. Every day with Lauren seemed to be an incredible day, Jake thought. It didn't matter that she was still planning to move away. He didn't think she'd be on the other side of the country though, so he expected that they could get together occasionally.

After her decision, they'd spent a lot of time laughing. Some of it was at nothing. They'd just look at each other and suddenly burst into gales of joy. Jake had never done that before—with anyone.

He remembered a time when there was sadness in Lauren's eyes. It was missing now.

He hoped he'd been part of the reason for that. She'd been a lot of the reason he could laugh again—focus on a future.

Lauren was sitting on the piano bench. She didn't play much, but she ran her hands across the keys just for the sound. Jake suddenly had an idea he wanted to test.

He walked over and sat down next to her.

"Want to play?" she asked, running an arpeggio over the keys.

"Not with one hand."

She cut her eyes at him. He'd done many things with one hand that he never thought he could do, including playing tennis, driving a car and typing on his computer.

He placed his left hand on the keys and looked at the open sheets she had on the music rack. A moderate-level arrangement of "Für Elise."

"This was one of the first pieces I learned to play."

"I'll play the right hand. You play the left," Lauren encouraged.

"Fair warning, I haven't played in years," he said. "I don't even think I can still sight-read."

"Try it." Lauren grinned at him.

Jake had ceased to tell her things he could not do. She'd argue and he'd have to try it anyway. He looked at the sheet music and wondered if she'd chosen this piece because it wasn't very complicated.

He practiced a few measures, then went back and did them again. On the third try, she joined him.

"That was good. Let's do it again," she said.

Jake was surprised he could do it especially since they kept the rhythm the way it was written.

When they got to the end, Lauren twisted on the seat. "You did it," she said and hugged him.

Jake immediately reacted and he hugged her too, although one-handedly. When she pulled away, he raked his hand over her back. Lauren laughed.

"You're ticklish," Jake said and opened and closed his fingers rapidly against her dress.

"I'll get you back for this." Lauren laughed some more.

He reached over and tickled her side. She laughed and tried to move away. Jake caught her and continued tickling her. Lauren laughed, twisting as she tried to free herself. Jake laughed too. The sound rose to the ceiling as the two tussled. Slipping off the bench, they fell softly to the floor, both of them still laughing. Jake stopped tickling her for a second, then started again. Lauren breathed hard, trying to stop laughing at the same time.

Neither of them heard the key go in the lock or the door to the apartment opening and closing. Finally, Lauren got away from him, backpedaling on hands and feet. Her laughter didn't stop, but it decreased. Jake caught her. He would have tickled her again, but he spied someone else in the apartment.

Both of them looked up.

"Cal!" Jake said.

"Caleb?" Lauren said.

The two of them spoke at the same time.

"What are you doing here?" Jake asked.

Cal's eyebrows nearly touched the ceiling. "Obviously, I'm interrupting something."

Lauren got to her feet, brushing her clothes off as if she'd picked up lint from the floor. Jake got up too.

"You're not interrupting anything," Jake said. "We were just horsing around."

"I see." Cal's tone meant he was reading more into their fooling around than was necessary.

Jake glanced at Lauren. Her face was a dark shade of red. Her hands twitched. She clasped them together to keep them from moving. Jake knew what this looked like to Cal. The truth was they were just having some fun.

"Lauren, would you leave us?" Jake said.

She nodded and went to the media room.

"What are you doing here?" Jake asked his brother as soon as Lauren closed the door.

"Technically, I'm here for a conference, but I thought I'd drop in and see how you were doing. Clearly, I should have called first or at least knocked on the door."

"It wasn't like that. We were just horsing around. There's nothing going on, as I've told you in the past."

"I'm not here to judge you, Jake. I'm sorry there isn't something going on."

"What?"

"You need someone," Cal said. "Maybe you could do a little more than just horsing around."

Both brothers laughed and man-hugged. Cal came farther into the room.

"So, how have you been?" Cal asked. "You look like a different person."

"I'm better than I was before you left."

"I see Lauren is having a positive effect on you."

"How long are you going to be here?"

"A couple of days. I fly back right after the conference on Friday."

"I see you have your suitcase. You're staying here, I assume."

"Just for tonight. The conference is in Philly. I thought maybe you and I could have dinner."

"Fine."

Jake was sure his brother didn't think he was willing to be seen in public. Cal had hired Lauren, but at the time he had no idea how persuasive she could be. And Jake was no longer conscious of people staring at him. In fact, a lot of it had been in his mind. This was New York. No one cared what he looked like. Lauren and her costumes had been proof positive of that.

PINS AND NEEDLES pricked Lauren's skin after the two brothers left for the night. She hoped Caleb wouldn't slip and say something to Jake that would show her hand. She was restless, unable to focus on anything. She walked around the apartment, picking up a book and putting it down. She went through the hundred channels on the television, but found nothing to watch.

Finally, she called Amy. It was her late night to work. Lauren agreed to meet her at her office and they would go for a drink afterward. She got there half an hour early.

The place was packed with people. No way was the office going to close on time.

Lauren waited ten minutes before she had to move.

"Amy, can I help?"

Amy looked confused. "Dr.—"

"I won't do any medicine, although my license is still valid. I'll help with triage and vitals."

"Let me check."

Amy went away and came back almost instantly. She nodded at Lauren and handed her a white coat. "Use room two."

It felt good to be a doctor again, to work with children, to watch the faces of parents who were happy to find out their child's hurt was simple to relieve. Lauren didn't overstep her boundaries. She checked for fevers and asked questions of the parents and children, some of whom were familiar to her. Then she passed the information on to the doctors. Traffic moved smoothly through the rooms.

With Lauren helping out, Amy wasn't as stressed being on the front line of parents with sick children. The parents also lost some of the stress of waiting. It took a little more than an hour and forty minutes before the last patient was out the door.

"Thank you," Amy said as she locked the door and turned the outside light off.

"Is it always like this on your late night?"

She nodded. "Most nights it's busy, but on the late night, the place is standing room only."

The doctors from the group came out to thank Lauren. Her feeling of usefulness overflowed.

"I was happy to do it," she said. "Although there were times when I wanted to go the full route of diagnosis and treatment. It was hard to stop at triage."

"You could consider coming back," Amy said.

Silence filled the room as if a sudden odor had been released. They all knew the story of Lauren's daughter.

"Not yet," Lauren said.

"Well," one of the doctors said, "if you want to think about it, I'm sure we'd be open to some negotiations."

"You may only need another nurse," Lauren offered. "That's the role I played tonight."

She knew she couldn't commit to working in the office. Not on a full-time or even a part-time basis. That place, that practice was her past, and she was all about her future. She'd made some big strides and didn't want to risk falling backward. That didn't mean she wouldn't plan to begin her medical career somewhere else.

Tonight had shown Lauren that she really loved medicine and that she had to return to it. When Jake was on his feet and she'd decided where she wanted to settle, she'd be quick to find a medical practice to join.

It took another half hour to clean up everything, but finally she and Amy were on their way for that drink.

"Things must be really bad if you need a drink," Amy said when they were seated at the bar and the bartender had set a piña colada in front of her. Amy ordered a nonalcoholic version of the same.

"I have to work tomorrow," Amy explained.

It might be a workday tomorrow, but the restaurant was packed. Nearly all the tables and bar stools were occupied on a night when there was no major sports game.

"Jake's brother showed up unexpectedly today."

Amy stopped with the glass halfway to her mouth. "The brother who hired you?"

"The same." Lauren nodded.

"Where are they?"

"Out to dinner and they might be talking about me. I'm afraid Caleb might forget that Jake doesn't know I'm a doctor. He also doesn't know that I regularly report to Caleb on his progress."

"He can't be angry if he finds out. Look how much you've helped him."

"I know, but he's a very stubborn man. I don't want him to crawl back into himself if he discovers both Caleb and I have hidden secrets from him."

"Like I said, you need to tell him the truth." Amy repeated a statement she'd made more than once.

The bartender put a plate of wings in front of them. Amy hadn't eaten since lunch and had ordered food. As soon as Lauren saw it, she was incredibly hungry. Together, they shared the wings and ordered more drinks.

"You can't do anything about it except worry, and that will do you no good. How long is Caleb staying?"

"Just tonight."

"That's a plus," she said. "Less time for them to talk. And if I were you, I'd try to stay out of their company when it's the two of them."

Amy was right. The two stayed out until eleven when Amy said she had to go home. "Tomorrow will arrive earlier than I want it to."

They left the bar, hugged good-night and each took a taxi. Lauren's head was reeling when she stepped out of the car. Her eyes didn't want to remain open. The combination of the drinks and her worry had made her extremely tired. She got in the elevator and turned to push the button for the top floor. The doors began to close. Suddenly a hand appeared and the doors opened.

Jake and Caleb stood there.

CHAPTER FIFTEEN

LAUREN HAD THE overwhelming need to
laugh. She'd been trying to avoid these two
men and here she was in an elevator with
them. She grinned slightly, trying not to
burst into full-fledged hysterics. The ride
seemed endless and Lauren couldn't hold the
mirth back. She snorted. Both men looked
at her.

"Are you all right?" Jake asked.

She said yes, but her head was shaking no.

"Lauren?" Caleb stepped closer, looking
concerned.

Lauren held her breath, willing the elevator to get to the top floor. The building had
only ten stories. She couldn't help it. She
started to giggle.

"Lauren, have you been drinking?" Jake
asked.

Lauren burst out laughing. The elevator
doors opened and she bolted from them,

hurrying down a hallway that was moving side to side. Miraculously, her key fit on the first try. Not waiting for the men behind her, she entered the apartment and, as fast as she could, started up the stairs to the bedroom level. The stairs seemed to work like an escalator that was going the wrong way. Each step up felt like two more down.

She heard the door open behind her as she grasped the handrail and pulled herself up. Lauren had to stand still a moment while the room stopped reeling. How much had she drunk? She couldn't remember if it was three or four cocktails. Suddenly, the image of the hallway veered one way and then the other, before it melded into one and she got to her room and closed the door. She switched the lock and collapsed onto the bed.

When she woke, it was still dark, but the illuminated numbers on the clock read five forty. She was still in her clothes and shoes and lying across the bedcovers. She pushed herself up and grabbed her head. It throbbed as if a jackhammer was inside. Closing her eyes, she waited several seconds, hoping the pain would ease. Her mouth felt like it was full of sand.

Had she ever felt this bad? Why hadn't Amy stopped those drinks from coming? Lauren slid off the bed. She needed to talk to Caleb before he left.

And without Jake.

Taking a moment to clean her teeth, she poked her head out of her room and checked for the two brothers. Neither one was in the visible space on the first floor. Lauren tiptoed down the steps and left the apartment. She went to the first floor and waited by the elevators. Caleb had to come down soon. She knew he was leaving early. She hoped when he appeared he'd be alone.

Lauren didn't have to wait long. Caleb exited the elevator with his suitcase in his hand.

"Caleb," she called, her voice a stage whisper.

He turned to face her. "Lauren, what are you doing here?" His smile was wide. "I hope you're feeling better."

"Not much," she said. "I wanted to ask you about Jake."

"Jake is so much better than when I left.

You're doing a wonderful job. Jake's even gained some of his weight back and he's happier than I've seen him since the accident."

Lauren was relieved. "You didn't tell him that I'm a doctor?"

"It never came up."

"I want to tell him," she said.

"That's up to you."

Caleb didn't offer any other opinion. Lauren had reservations. She and Jake were doing well as friends and she valued that. She felt she could talk to him about anything, except who she really was. And he talked to her too. He'd told her about his life, his fiancée, the explosion.

"I have to go now," Caleb said.

A car appeared outside the door.

"Enjoy your conference," she said.

"Thanks and don't look so worried. Jake likes you. You're good for him."

With that he went through the door. Lauren watched him get in the car. A woman was driving. The car pulled through the arched portico and she couldn't see which way it turned. For the moment, she felt safe. Jake didn't know who she was. He might ask her about her actions of the night before. Lauren wasn't sure she could explain it. At least not in a coherent manner.

It was ironic that the two people she was trying to avoid had caught her as if she was sneaking in from a clandestine meeting. She couldn't help the giggle that bubbled up inside her. She wondered what Jake thought of her after seeing her in the elevator. What would he ask her when he showed up for breakfast?

Lauren couldn't go back to sleep. And Jake didn't come down for breakfast at the usual time. He'd had a long night out, as had she, but he didn't have as many piña coladas. By the time he started down the stairs, Lauren had been pacing for nearly an hour. Her headache was no better than it had been when she got out of bed.

Jake passed her without a word. He went into the kitchen. Lauren felt as if he was angry with her. She had to explain, although she didn't know what to say. She shouldn't have drunk all that alcohol. She ordered the drinks because they tasted good and she'd been more concerned about Jake and Caleb's possible discussions than the number of glasses put in front of her.

The kitchen door opened and Jake came back in. Lauren's heart accelerated and she nearly jumped at his appearance.

"Drink this?" he said, holding a glass with a red liquid in it.

"What is it?"

"It's for your hangover."

She didn't ask if it was obvious that she had one. She knew her face showed the pain that was in her head. She drank the liquid. It didn't taste bad. It had a lot of tomato juice in it.

"Will this help?" she asked.

"Probably not. The best thing you could do is go back to bed."

She sat down. "Sleep it off."

"Essentially, yes," Jake said.

Sleep sounded like a good idea. Before Jake came down, she'd been too fidgety to sleep, but now she suddenly craved it. But Lauren couldn't go just yet. She needed to explain her actions.

"Jake, I apologize. I never intended—"

"Stop," he said, raising his hand. "Your time is your time. You have the right to do whatever you want when you're not working."

"But your brother was here and—"

"And he didn't judge you either. In fact, he thought you were a little funny."

"Funny," Lauren objected, then held her head. "I think I will get some rest."

LAUREN DIDN'T GO to sleep immediately. She had something important to do and even with a headache she could get it done only when Jake was not around or she'd gone to her room for the night.

She looked with pride at the finished pop-up book. The first one she'd done all those years ago took her hours to complete and was very basic. *Amateurish* was a better word. It was only a single page with a tree that stood up when it was opened. It looked like a three-year-old made it with globs of glue, construction paper that was too thick and double-stick tape that was too weak to hold. Yet Lauren kept it to remind her how far she'd come.

Her second effort wasn't much better, but it took only an hour to make. Thankfully, she'd progressed over the years and her collection now had very complicated designs.

Like him, the book she'd been making for Jake's birthday present was very complex. Lauren spent two weeks to cut the paper shapes, write the text and put the book together using the supplies she'd purchased in DC. Now if she could just pull off the party without his knowledge.

After she'd gotten the last piece in place and the story was done, Lauren succumbed to her headache and went to sleep. She woke without remembering if she dreamed anything. She was thirsty and hungry and thankfully her headache was gone.

Jake wasn't in the apartment when she went to the kitchen. She drank an entire bottle of water in only a few swallows. Then she took a second bottle and headed out. She wondered where he was. Although she was no longer concerned about his health or him being in pain, it was rare for him to leave without telling her where he was going.

However, she used the time efficiently. His birthday was tomorrow and she had a few details to put in place. She hoped he'd be happy with what she'd made for him.

With Jake, she was still on pins and needles as to what his reaction would be. This had to be positive. It had to go well.

LAUREN WAS USUALLY up before Jake came down to breakfast. Finally the day had arrived. Jake hadn't mentioned a thing about his birthday. Still she had it covered. She enjoyed celebrating her birthday. She didn't know how Jake felt about his. If it hadn't been for Caleb mentioning it, Lauren was sure Jake would have let it go by unnoticed. But he was getting a party anyway.

She'd invited two of the doctors he consulted with and Amy. Inevitably, the conversation would be medical. But hopefully they'd have stories to share and lots of other things to talk about.

Lauren was amazed she'd managed to keep the party a secret. She'd shared her plans with the housekeeper, who was on board from the beginning. She took care of all the food, while Lauren invited the guests and finished her present.

As Jake went to take a shower, believing they were going out to dinner, Lauren decorated the table with a centerpiece of birthday cards, flowers and candles.

The guests arrived on time.

"Surprise!" they shouted when Jake stepped into the upstairs hall.

Lauren felt his eyes connect with hers. For a moment, she held her breath. Then Jake smiled.

"Wow!" Amy said close to Lauren's ear. "He's gorgeous."

Lauren shot her a stop-that look.

"What's this?" Jake asked.

"Happy birthday," Dr. Chase said.

Jake looked at Lauren. "How'd you know it was my birthday?"

"The internet," she said. "You've got a bio out there."

Jake turned to the group. He glanced at the table settings. "I guess we aren't going out to dinner."

Everyone laughed. Lauren introduced Amy as a colleague whom she used to work with. Everyone else knew each other.

Lauren and the housekeeper served drinks while Jake and the doctors mingled. As predicted, they immediately started tossing round medical terminology. Lauren again reminded herself not to reveal that she had any medical knowledge. Jake put his arm out and she moved toward him. He didn't embrace her.

"Why don't we sit down?"

As the group moved to the table, the lobby phone rang. It was rare for that to happen. Since she'd been there, that phone had never rung. Lauren was closest to it and she picked up the receiver. "Hello?"

"Dr. Masters has a guest in the lobby. But she is not on the list."

"Who is it?" Lauren asked.

"Dr. Ingraham. Dr. Paula Ingraham."

Lauren froze when she heard Paula's voice in the background repeating her name. What was she doing here? She had not been invited.

"It's his birthday. I only want to deliver his present."

She was talking to the concierge. Lauren could hear the muffled sound, but the words were clear as if she was shouting in order to be heard through the receiver.

"Have her come up," Lauren said.

"Who is it?" Jake whispered.

"Dr. Ingram."

"You invited her?"

Lauren shook her head.

The doorbell rang a moment later. Jake answered it and she swept into the room like a sudden wind. She went straight into Jake's arms and kissed his cheek. She would have kissed his lips, but he turned his head at the same moment and she missed.

"Paula, this is a surprise," Jake said.

"Happy birthday. I had to bring this by. I knew you'd want it."

Looking past him and into the room, she saw the gathering. "Oh, you're having a party."

Instead of doing what any uninvited guest would do, apologize for the interruption and back out the door, she entered the room as if her invitation had been lost in the mail.

"Dr. Chase, Dr. Faris, I didn't know you were coming."

Again, Lauren noticed that Paula was making it appear that she was expected.

"Sorry to be late, but isn't that a woman's prerogative?" She laughed, but no one else did.

"Let me get you a drink," Lauren offered.

"I'll do it," Jake said. He put the box she'd

brought on the table by the door and led her to the drinks cart that Lauren had set up.

Lauren glanced at him and understood that his action was to help her, not Paula Ingram. Taking the opportunity, Lauren went to the kitchen and signaled the housekeeper to set another place at the table. Thankfully, the other guests had not gotten to the table yet, so no one had noticed that there was no place setting for a sixth guest.

The night couldn't have gone any worse. Paula dominated the conversation, speaking a little too loud and bringing everything back to her or her opinion. Her eyes were always on Jake as if they were compelled to be there like a magnetic compass pointing north. Lauren kept up conversations with the two doctors and Amy.

It was hard for Lauren to keep her mind on what they were saying. When they lapsed into medicine, she had to remain quiet, even though she was dying to contribute.

Dr. Chase apologized for his lapse of manners.

"No apology needed," Lauren said. "I'm glad you and Jake are able to communicate on medical issues."

"He's good. We need him back at the hospital," Dr. Faris said.

"I'm on that," she whispered conspiratorially. "I think in the next few weeks we can convince him to work at the hospital."

"That would be very helpful."

The housekeeper served dessert and coffee and Amy whispered to her, "Who is she?"

Dr. Faris heard the question and answered. "She's a woman who thinks she can win Jake." He paused and glanced at Lauren. "But—" he leaned close to her "—she hasn't seen how Jake looks at Lauren."

Amy smiled. Lauren knew her friend had intimated that there was a romance going on between her and Jake. While it wasn't the truth, it wasn't a total lie either. Lauren had fallen for Jake and she didn't appreciate the way Dr. Ingram was all over him, but there was nothing she could say. Jake was a grown man. He had to make his choice. But Lauren had never added her name to a list of possibilities. Obviously, Paula had. There was no mistaking her intent.

"Dr. Faris," Lauren said.

"Doug," he said.

"Doug, I'm his caretaker for the moment. Jake and I have no relationship."

The doctor sipped his coffee, his eyes never leaving hers.

"You have to open my present." Paula's voice was high and intended for the entire table to hear.

"Let's move to the living room," Lauren suggested.

Everyone got up and started for the other room.

"How is she as a doctor?" Amy asked.

"Surprisingly competent," Dr. Faris replied.

But her intentions regarding Jake had nothing to do with medicine, Lauren thought.

Paula retrieved the large box from the table and brought it to the living room. She presented it like a cure for cancer. Jake tried to take it in his one hand, but it teetered and fell sideways. Amy caught it.

"Let me help," she said.

Lauren saw the look that Amy threw her. She was putting herself between Jake and Dr. Ingram. Jake tore the paper away and Amy pulled the flap up. She tilted the box so he could see inside. Jake reached in and pulled out a wine-colored cashmere robe with his initials monogrammed in bright white stitches.

Amy stood up and backed away. "I'll bet she has one just like it with her initials on it," she said under her breath.

Lauren smirked and started to laugh behind her hand.

"What'd you get him?" Amy asked.

Before she could answer, Paula's comment caught their attention.

"Try it on," she said. She grabbed the robe and stood up holding it ready for him to slip his arms in.

"Paula." Dr. Chase stopped her. "Not now. He can do that in private."

"It's only a robe," she said. "It's not like I'm asking him to undress."

"Not now," he said again. This time his tone was like a father speaking to a child.

Paula backed down.

"I'll put this away," Lauren said.

Lauren moved the robe, box and the wrapping paper debris to the dining room and then returned.

"More coffee, anyone?" she asked.

The two doctors refused. Amy accepted.

"What a great apartment," Paula said. "These windows are magnificent."

Paula was not to be put off. She walked up to the windows and looked out.

"It must be easy to come home to all this," she said.

"The apartment has been in my family all my life. My grandmother used to own it," Jake said.

Amy came up to Lauren. "Where did you find her?"

"I didn't. She shouted her way in."

"And she's latched onto Jake like a mountain climber with a sharp spike."

Lauren couldn't help laughing. Amy joined her.

The party went on until midnight. Of course, Paula wanted to stay on after everyone else had left, but Dr. Chase stopped her.

"Paula, I have a car. I'm happy to drop you off. Amy, would you like to join us?"

With kisses and handshakes all around, the group left.

"Wow!" Jake said as he plopped down on the sofa. "That was the worst birthday party I've ever had."

"I'm sorry," Lauren said, sitting on the

table in front of him. "I tried so hard to make it a memorable one."

"Oh, it was." Jake leaned forward and took both of her hands in his one. He started to laugh.

"What's so funny?"

"Your face when I pulled that robe out of the box."

Lauren smiled. She imagined what she looked like, but it couldn't compete with the way she must have looked when Paula asked him to try it on. Jake's hand was warm holding hers, but she had tensed when she thought he might actually slip on Paula's gift.

"Speaking of gifts, I have one for you, although it can't compete with a personalized robe."

Both of them laughed again. Lauren got up and went to the kitchen, where she'd hidden the present. Returning, she handed him a box wrapped in black and silver paper with a huge silver bow on top.

"Where's Amy when you need her?" he said.

Lauren took the box and held it while Jake pulled the ribbon free and slit the paper.

Lauren opened the flaps and Jake reached inside.

"What is this?" he said. "It's not large enough to be a robe."

Lauren kept her face straight. She hoped he liked it.

"It's a book," he said, placing it on his knees. *"Yes, I Can,"* he read the title. "Am I running for president and this is my campaign manual?"

Lauren shook her head.

He opened the book and the page popped up.

"It's a pop-up book," he said eagerly. "This is beautiful." He read the text and looked at the pop-ups. By the third page, he looked at her. "This is our story."

"It's your story," she said.

The book showed the apartment with the large windows and the New York skyline outside. All their activities were featured, starting with their picnic in the park. Lauren had a hard time finding a photo of Jake that she could use. She'd come across professional shots, and some of Jake as the extreme sports enthusiast he'd been, but few of them reflected the man that he was now.

"Everything is here," he said. "My first time driving. Even the Washington, DC, trip and tonight's party." He looked up at her. "Paula is missing."

"She was a surprise, but if you want me to add her…"

"Absolutely not," he said without hesitating. Looking down at the book again, he waved his hand. "This might not have been the best party, but this is the best present I've ever received. Thank you."

Lauren smiled. Jake leaned forward and kissed her on the cheek. He moved back not far enough. He was still in her personal space, their faces close.

"Happy birthday," she whispered.

"The happiest," he said and his mouth touched hers. Lauren moved forward for a full kiss.

THE PARK LOOKED greener to Lauren during the last week of August. She thought she'd be gone by now, but here she was almost three months later, still staying in the apartment with Jake. He was making progress and selfishly she attributed it to her being there. They'd expanded their drives with greater distances, spending the day antiquing in Pennsylvania or exploring quaint inns in Massachusetts. But today they were walking in the park. It was like the beginning, but without the drama.

Lauren knew exactly when the change occurred. She'd been back to visit Naliani several times alone. Leaving, she wasn't happy, but she was no longer bereft.

Returning to the apartment building, Jake checked his mail and they rode up in the elevator together. "I have a surprise for you," he said, upon opening the door.

"Surprise?" Lauren's heart lifted. She looked at the mail in his hand. He hadn't gone through the envelopes. Most were medical journals or magazines.

"Saturday is your day off. Would you like to go out?"

"We go out every day."

"This time we could have dinner and then go to a play."

"You mean like a date?" she asked.

"Are you opposed to going on a date with me?" He put the mail on the table.

"No," she said.

"I have tickets to *Mary Poppins* on Broadway and I thought you'd like to see it with me."

Lauren put her hand over her mouth to hide the bubble of laughter that threatened to burst. It worked for only a few seconds before she was laughing. Jake started to laugh with her until the two of them were struggling for breath.

"I suppose…" Lauren began sucking air into her lungs. "I suppose it's the perfect musical. Shall I dress the part?"

"You did leave the carpetbag here."

On Saturday night as Lauren stepped into the limousine that Jake ordered, she wasn't dressed as any nanny. Her outfit wasn't quite special occasion, but the night was special to her and the dress she wore was a knockout shade of red. Jake wore a dark suit and white shirt. The contrast between the clothes and his skin was stark. Many of their day trips in the sun had left him with a tan and gentle highlights to his dark hair.

Lauren watched women turning to look at him as they entered the restaurant. She felt slightly regal at the fact that he was with her.

"Did you notice all the stares?"

"Yes, I might have to fight all the guys who ogled you."

"They didn't ogle me. It was the women looking at *you*."

He glanced around as if he hadn't noticed. Lauren wasn't sure if he hadn't seen the way his entrance had attracted attention. Maybe he was so used to it that it no longer seemed like a novelty. He was a very attractive man.

"No one seems to be looking now."

Lauren hid her smile as the waiter handed her a large menu. After she ordered, she asked, "Have you seen *Mary Poppins* before?"

"I haven't watched many musicals."

"You do know they sing in this *musical*?" she teased. "More than likely it will begin with a song, end with a song and have singing throughout."

"You're playing with me," he said, teasingly.

Lauren just lifted an eyebrow. "Seriously, you've never seen the play or movie?"

"Never," he said. "But I know someone who could probably give me a rundown, complete with songs and dancing."

He could barely get the sentence out

without laughing. Lauren liked hearing his laugh. This Jake Masters was miles away from the angry young man she'd met on her first day. He was almost as playful and happy as the college student who sat in front of her in physics class.

Their meals arrived and for a few moments they were quiet, enjoying the flavor of the food. Lauren hadn't been on a date in months and being with Jake felt good. She was comfortable with him. She'd gone through some of his bad days, been witness to his volatile moods and been the confidante he shared his private thoughts with. And now he was taking her out on a date.

With all she knew about him, there was very little he knew about her. She'd told him about Naliani, and she knew he was instrumental in helping her deal with the loss of her child, but he didn't know a particular detail about her and she needed to tell him.

By the time they were having coffee, Lauren knew the moment had come. She needed to tell him tonight. That meant this might be the last time she saw Jake. Cal was due to return soon. Jake was continuing his consulting and eventually he would work at the hospital again. She knew he really wanted to return to medicine and he was ready. She was sure his arm wouldn't be a problem for the doctors or the patients. As long as he didn't have to perform surgery, he could still work as a doctor. Her job was done. Lauren hadn't thought of it when Jake asked her out, but this date was probably the crowning moment of her time with him. Soon she'd turn back into the former college acquaintance he once knew and disappear from his life.

He had to know the truth about her. "Jake."

He looked up with a smile in his eyes. Lauren almost lost her nerve. She swallowed and forced herself to speak. "There's something I need to talk to you about."

"Okay."

He was still smiling. She opened her mouth to say something just as the waiter came over.

"Curtain in half an hour," he said, then moved to the next table.

Jake looked at her. "We can talk after the play."

As she'd told Jake, the production opened with a song. They sat together in the eighth row center and for two hours were taken to a world of chimney sweeps, precocious children and the love of family. Lauren couldn't stop thoughts of Naliani from forming when she saw the little girl in the play. Almost every little girl had once made her think of her daughter. It was the reason she sold her practice. She'd needed time away from children. The pain was too great, too raw. But now, she watched the little girl, remembered Naliani with love in her heart, but without the emotions that once destroyed her.

When the last song was sung and the audience was on its feet applauding, Jake was up too. With his left hand, he patted his right.

"You liked it," Lauren stated as they joined the crowd in the aisles and headed for the exit.

"It had its moments."

She knew he was kidding. "I heard you humming some of the songs."

"I might have learned a chorus or two."

Lauren squeezed his arm. "Where are we going now?" she asked.

"How about we go for drinks and a little music? Not Broadway music." He turned and looked at her. The warmth she felt from it was unforgettable.

"That sounds fine." She didn't want the evening to end.

Out on the street, they looked for their limousine among the many waiting at curbside. Seeing it, Jake turned her toward it. In that instant her past leapt out at her.

"Dr. Graves."

Lauren couldn't help but turn. Since she was on her way to becoming a doctor before she married Richard, she'd kept her maiden name when it came to her profession. In her practice, she was always called Dr. Graves. A woman was rushing toward her. Someone she recognized. It was Mrs. Rawlins, Becky Rawlins's mother. Following her was a man who had to be the child's father. Lauren had never met him.

"Dr. Graves." Mrs. Rawlins stopped in front of her. "How are you? The nurse told us about your daughter."

"I'm doing well," Lauren said.

Mr. Rawlins caught up with his wife. She turned and introduced them. "This is the doctor who diagnosed what was wrong with Becky."

He shook hands with her and Lauren had no choice but to introduce Jake. She didn't want to look at him. She could feel the heat of his stare. Red that it was, she was surprised it didn't burn her skin.

"How is Becky doing?" Lauren asked.

"She's back to her old self. You'd never know she had surgery," Mr. Rawlins said. "We can't thank you enough."

"No need. I was happy she got the treatment she needed."

"Well, thank you again," Mr. Rawlins said. "We have to rush off now. We have a reservation for a late dinner."

"Good night." Mrs. Rawlins waved.

And now it was time to face Jake.

CHAPTER SIXTEEN

THE RIDE BACK to the apartment was silent, but the mood inside the limo was vastly different from the trip out. Jake sat next to her seething. Lauren knew she couldn't talk to him. Maybe when they reached the apartment, he'd have calmed down a bit, but she didn't put much hope in that.

The moment the limo stopped under the enclosed archway, he bounded out of the car and into the building. When Lauren entered the apartment minutes later, Jake was clearly upset. He paced back and forth and couldn't seem to bring himself to look at her.

"Doctor? You're a doctor?" he accused.

"Let me explain. It's what I wanted to tell you at dinner, but the waiter interrupted us."

"Oh, that's convenient. You've been here how long—three months—and you never found an appropriate moment to slip that little bit of information in?"

"I wanted to, but Caleb and I knew—"

"Cal!" Jake stopped pacing and glared at her. "Is he in on this too?"

Lauren said nothing.

"I should have known." He flung the words. "He did the background check. Handed it to me, but I never read it. I trusted him."

"Jake, listen. He was thinking of you."

"By deceiving me? By sending you here to spy on me."

"I never spied on you."

"Is that true? You didn't talk to my brother, give him progress reports on my condition? You didn't tell him I drove a car or that I was working with the hospital?"

Lauren did all those things. "You make it sound like I was doing something terrible. Caleb is concerned about you."

"I specifically told Cal I did not want any more doctors prodding me, and he finds you. And you're good."

He put his left hand over his heart. "And now I'm better. I can drive and I can work. I guess your job is done. You're no longer the keeper of secrets. You can leave any-time now."

"Jake!"

He turned and headed up the stairs. Lauren called after him, but he didn't stop and he didn't look back. The slamming of his bedroom door was as powerful a statement as if he'd closed it in her face.

Lauren walked slowly up the stairs. She knew this day would come. She knew it was time she left, but she wanted to go as a friend, not as an enemy.

Jake had told her to leave. If she could leave tonight, she would. But she had to pack and she didn't trust herself to drive. Not that she had anywhere to go except Amy's. And she wouldn't call Amy at this time of night and tell her she was moving in.

One more night in the apartment with Jake only a few doors away. She was unlikely to see him again. She'd take the image of him running up the steps and slamming the door as their last encounter.

Lauren pulled her suitcase from the closet and set it on the bed.

THE NIGHT HAD been one of her worst. Lauren hadn't slept at all. She'd tossed and turned reliving the argument with Jake. There was nothing she could say to defend herself. He was right about her having every opportunity to tell him that she was a doctor. But she'd promised Caleb that she wouldn't tell Jake that fact. Her job was to help Jake when he needed assistance, that she had helped to convince him to rejoin the world meant so much more.

Yes. She had done that.

But that was over now. Lauren was packed and ready to leave long before the sun rose, though she waited until daylight to open the door to the hall and slip out of her room.

She looked around for the last time. She loved this apartment. Being here, above the city, seeing its beauty, had felt an escape from the pain that was her constant companion. Being with Jake gave her a purpose. She had someone to concentrate on instead of spending her days and nights remembering her loss.

She adjusted the purse on her shoulder and opened the front door. She carried a single suitcase. All she had to account for her time with Jake was a small suitcase of clothes. Even the costumes fit inside. Lauren took one last look back. As she stepped into the hall, she felt like she was leaving part of herself behind. In fact, she'd lost her heart.

Her car was in the garage close to the building. After putting her case in the trunk, she got behind the wheel and started the engine. It wasn't like Jake's sports car. Hers was a Lexus, powerful but practical. Pulling out of the parking space, she looked up. She couldn't see anything. She wasn't even out of the neighborhood, but she wondered if Jake would notice she was gone. Maybe when his arm began to hurt again.

She'd miss him. She already missed him.

JAKE'S EYES WERE scratchy and his throat was parched. He'd been so angry when he left her at the bottom of the stairs. Sleep eluded him for hours. He'd finally fallen asleep as the sun was rising and slept only an hour. He hated arguing with Lauren, but how could she deceive him that way? And what about Cal? They'd both been in on it. He found the report on her that Cal had given to him and there was nothing in it stating she was a doctor. All the while she'd been with him, it was because she needed to monitor him. He should have recognized it. In hindsight, the clues were obvious. She pronounced medical terms correctly, while a layman would falter over them. She seemed to understand his feelings, know when he was in distress and exactly what to do for it. And he'd ignored it. The thought that these skills were signs of a trained medical professional never entered his mind.

Jake knew why. He'd been so impressed and intrigued by her. He liked talking to her and being with her. He'd miss her when she left. But before that, they had to have some kind of closure.

Dr. Lauren Graves, Lori to her friends. He'd looked her up on the internet. She was a prominent pediatrician. Though not a surgeon, the articles she wrote in the medical journals were numerous. He found her bio. She'd grown up in a small town in western Maryland, gone to Catholic University, then to Johns Hopkins Medical School. She'd done a residency at Brooklyn Pediatric Hospital and set up her own practice.

There were photos of the medical arts building where she had her offices and several of her with various hairstyles, but always the same smile. Jake softened a bit at seeing it. Then he snapped the cover of the computer closed and tried to sleep.

Showering and dressing took little time. Leaving his bedroom, he went down the steps, not knowing what he would say to Lauren when they came face-to-face. He could smell the coffee, so she was most likely in the kitchen, where they'd prepared meals together, cleaned up together and talked about their days. On his way to the kitchen, he saw the bag by the door. As if it were a living thing, Jake stopped. His body seemed to turn to ice as a thought slipped into his mind that couldn't be true.

It was the carpetbag Lauren had used with her nanny costume. It sat sadly on its own as if it had been left behind on purpose. He almost expected it to disappear before his eyes.

"Lauren," he called, looking up. There was no reply and her door was ajar. "Lauren," he called louder and again no reply. He suddenly had the feeling that he was alone. She was not upstairs. He took two steps toward the stairs and was suddenly running. He kept calling her name as he bounded up the staircase.

Pushing the door wide open, he stopped. The room was perfect. The bed was made. The curtains allowed the bright morning sunlight to stream through the room.

But Lauren was not present.

The soft fragrance of lilac hung in the air, a reminder that she hadn't been a figment of his imagination. The dresser was cleared of her things. One by one he pulled the drawers out. Everything she owned was gone. The same with the closet. Only empty hangers were there as if this had been a hotel room and her stay had ended.

"The lilacs," he said out loud. The scent lingered. "She has to be close."

Jake left the apartment at a dead run. The garage where she parked her car was down the street. He didn't take time to worry about his clothing or the fact that he had no shoes on. He punched the elevator button over and over, forcing the action to make it come faster. He got inside, drumming his fingers on the railing as the small car descended to the ground floor. As soon as the elevator doors opened, he headed to the garage.

He had to find Lauren. He needed to tell

her to stay. He had to let her know he'd fallen in love with her, and despite the fact that she had kept her true profession from him, he wanted her to stay. He needed her like he needed to breathe.

The garage was underground and he didn't know what level she was on. He ran down the ramp and started searching level by level, listening for the sound of a car. He heard one and headed in the direction of the purring engine. The car was moving fast when he sighted it. And it was heading straight for him.

The driver hit the brake hard. Jake jumped out of the way. The car swerved and started to fishtail. He jumped out of the way as it plowed into a support pole. The engine immediately began to hiss. Jake heard the exploding air bag as it deployed. Running as hard as he could, he reached the vehicle.

Lauren sat slumped against the driver's bag. Without thinking, Jake yanked the car door open and caught Lauren in both hands as her body began to slide sideways.

It was only when he'd pulled his cell phone out and dialed 9-1-1 that he realized he was using his right hand.

WHY HADN'T JAKE ever noticed that the bright white of hospital sheets made the patient look pale? Lauren hadn't come to in the car. Jake had horrible moments waiting for the ambulance. Then the police and EMTs forced him to back away while they took care of getting Lauren out of the car and on the way to the hospital. Not allowed to ride with them, he followed in his own car, the same car Lauren had forced him to drive. Only this time he was using both hands.

Jake held her hand as she lay recovering from surgery. She'd been asleep all day and night. Several nurses had come in to monitor her, and asked him to leave. He refused. He wanted to be there when she opened her eyes. He wanted to apologize and tell her how much she meant to him. He wanted to tell her about his arm. She should be the first to know. She'd believed that he could eventually move it. She'd also coaxed him into believing that if motion never returned, there were things he could still do and be satisfied doing them. Of course, the doctors, therapists and nurses he'd seen had gotten there ahead of Lauren with that knowledge. She was taken to Jake's former hospital, and had not wakened before she had to go to surgery.

Many of the doctors knew Jake and urged him to let them examine his arm. He refused. Only when Lauren woke, and they talked, would he do it. He knew she would tell him he should have been examined already. But he wanted to see her conscious first.

When the hospital room door opened, Jake turned, expecting to find another nurse, but there was someone else coming in. *Amy.* He remembered her from the party that had Lauren organized for his birthday. She looked worried and harried, and Jake could understand why. She was breathing hard and her eyes moved from him to Lauren and back again.

"Jake," she said.

He nodded.

Coming forward, she extended her hand and Jake took it. She didn't let go, but looked down and kept holding on to him.

"I thought…" She trailed off.

"Movement only came back yesterday," he said, leaving out the circumstances that led to it happening.

Dropping his hand, she said, "The hospital called me."

"I'm sorry I didn't think of it. I've just been so focused on Lauren." *Should he try to contact her ex-husband?*

"How is Lauren doing?"

Jake nodded. "She's doing okay. Surgery went well. She's sleeping."

"Is she going to be all right?"

"That's the prognosis."

Amy seemed to relax at that. She walked around the bed and looked down. "How long before she wakes up?"

"I'm not sure."

"Excuse me for saying it, but you look like you've been here a long while."

"Since they brought her in."

"I'm here now and I'll stay for a few hours. You can go and get some sleep."

Jake appreciated the offer, and even though he admitted he probably did look bad, he wasn't about to go. "I'm all right," he said.

"I've heard that before. You need rest."

"My sentiments exactly."

They both turned to see who had entered the room.

"You've been here a while," Dr. Chase said. "It's time we looked at that arm. Plus, your test results are still here, waiting for you. Let's go over them."

Jake knew the ramifications of what he was doing. He also knew things could go either way. He could revert to nonuse or he could regain it totally. He glanced at Lauren, who looked the same. She probably wouldn't wake until he returned.

"I promise, if she wakes up, they'll come and get us," Dr. Chase said.

"She'd want you to go," Amy whispered so only he could hear.

Jake knew she was right.

CHAPTER SEVENTEEN

LAUREN MOANED AND opened her eyes. She closed them immediately. Everything hurt, but mainly it was her head. The accident.

"Jake," she murmured.

"I'm here."

She heard his voice, tried to turn her head, but the pain stopped her. It was intense, unlike anything she'd felt before. Hands touched her shoulders.

"You're all right," Jake soothed. "Lie still. I'll get someone."

"Are you…" She tried to speak through the pain. "Did I hit you?"

"I'm fine. I'm better than fine," he said. She heard the emotion in his voice, even though her eyes were closed.

The door opened and she heard the rustle of feet coming toward her. She knew the sound.

"Dr. Masters, we'll have to ask you to leave," an official no-nonsense voice told him.

Lauren felt the pressure of his hand against her shoulder. He released it and she thought she was being abandoned.

"I'll be right outside the door," he said.

Lauren would have smiled, if the pain in her head wasn't so awful.

When asked how she felt, she told them about the pain and almost immediately it subsided. Lauren could think more clearly with the pain no longer having such a hold of her. She realized the nurse must have added something to her IV.

Her questions were answered by the nurse, who explained which hospital she was in, that she was the only victim of the accident and that she'd been in the hospital overnight.

The doctor explained that she'd had surgery for internal bleeding, but they expected no lasting complications.

"When can I go home?" she asked.

"Give it a day or two," the doctor replied.

Lauren tried to remain calm. She wouldn't be able to find a new place to live and work as soon as she expected. Jake was fine.

She hadn't hurt him. Recovery from internal bleeding could take weeks before her strength returned. She was no longer welcome at Jake's and now that he knew she was a doctor, he likely wouldn't speak to her ever again.

She'd never regret a single moment of the time she spent getting to know him.

Amy came in, rushing to Lauren's side. "How are you?" she asked.

"Better now that they gave me something for the pain."

"Did they say—"

She didn't get to finish. The door opened and Jake came in. Amy whispered that she had to leave, but she'd be back the next day.

Then she was alone with Jake.

LAUREN WAS ALMOST in tears looking at Jake. She was relieved that he was all right.

"I'm sorry," she said.

"Sorry for what?" He came to the bed where she lay. Lauren watched every step he took.

"I nearly killed you."

He smiled. "You didn't. I jumped in time. Shouldn't have been in your way in the first place. But forget about me, it's you we need to focus on here." He looked at her from head to toe.

Lauren didn't understand. She was having a hard time concentrating. Her headache was coming back.

"You must be tired," he said.

She didn't reply. She was tired. For some reason, she didn't seem to be able to stay awake more than a few minutes. It was probably the meds, she thought before yawning again.

"I'll leave now and come back tomorrow."

He bent over and kissed her forehead. Lauren looked up, wondering why he did that. Then he kissed her lightly on the mouth and leaned back. She licked her lips, drawing the taste of him inside.

Before she could say anything else, he was going out the door. And she was falling asleep again.

"LAUREN."

Opening her eyes at the sound of her name, she squinted, recognizing Amy.

"Hi, Amy." Her mind was fuzzy. Had she seen Amy today? How long had she been in the hospital? Lauren yawned. "What did they give me?" she asked no one in particular. Her eyes were heavy and she closed them.

When Lauren opened her eyes the next time, the room was empty and it was still dark outside. She was thirsty and her stomach felt tight. She reached down and felt the bandages. She wanted to see what the surgeon had done, but knew that wasn't something she should do. She lay back and pushed the call button.

Immediately, the door opened and a nurse came inside. "How do you feel, Dr. Graves?"

"Thirsty," she said.

The nurse poured her a small cup and used a straw to help her drink.

"Is Dr. Masters here?" She remembered seeing him. *How long ago was that?*

"He was discharged and left. He was here for a long time. I'm sure he'll be back."

But he didn't come back. Lauren didn't know who called her father, but he was there until she was discharged two days later with a long list of instructions. Amy picked them up and insisted she stay with her until she was well enough to be on her own.

Amy lived on the top floor of a Brooklyn brownstone built in the early twentieth century. It had high ceilings and a decent amount of space. She had remodeled much of it to suit her more modern taste.

Lauren's father stayed with a friend, but was constantly underfoot, fetching any and everything she needed. After the first day, Lauren was ready to be on her own, but she kept quiet about the administrations. She knew they were doing it out of love and didn't protest.

Lauren did wonder where Jake was and why he didn't come to see her. She remembered his running into the garage as she was leaving. What did he want? He'd been in the hospital when she woke up. Had he come to make sure she was all right before retreating into himself? Or was he still angry with her for not telling him the whole truth?

At breakfast on the third day, before Lauren's father arrived, she and Amy sat in the kitchen. Amy was preparing to go to work. She had a metal travel mug in her hand and was twisting the top on. Lauren was jealous, she still couldn't handle coffee yet.

"You know you can call him," she said.

Lauren looked up. They hadn't been talking about Jake, but he was suddenly the topic of conversation.

"What would I say?" she asked. "We'd had a fight. He said he never wanted to see me again."

"He may have said that, but the man in the waiting room and the one sitting by your bed throughout the day and night didn't look like he never wanted to see you again."

"Yet it's what he said."

Amy looked at her seriously. "Try giving him a call and asking."

"I can't do that."

"Then just say hello and let it go from there," Amy said.

Half an hour later, Lauren sat on the steps of the Brooklyn brownstone and took out her phone. Someone had turned it off when she was in the hospital and she hadn't reset it. When she powered it on, she had fifteen missed calls from Jake. Should she contact him? She looked at his number, wondering if she should hit the call button. He'd told her to leave his apartment, yet he'd stayed with her at the hospital. Then he left, but had tried to reach her. What should she infer from those actions? Did he want to know if she was all right? Was there something else?

She'd almost hit him with the car. He said he'd jumped out of the way, but what was he doing in the garage anyway? Had he come because she'd left or was there something else he wanted to say?

Amy was right. She should call him. But she wasn't going to do that. She had something else in mind, but she needed to act before her father arrived. Gathering her purse and running shoes, she set out for Jake's apartment. She'd laid his key on the piano when she left, so she had no access to the apartment if he wasn't there.

Mrs. Turner, the housekeeper, answered the door and had her purse over her shoulder. Lauren knew she was ready to leave, but a bright smile lit her face when she saw Lauren.

"Welcome home," she said.

A hopeful emotion was quickly replaced by one that said she didn't live here anymore.

"Is he here?"

"He's in the office."

Alone, Lauren looked around the apartment. Nothing had changed since she was last in the place, but she felt as if something was missing. She couldn't put a name to it. Was it that the room had no life? That even when she and Jake argued, there was still an energy to the place, which it now lacked.

Lauren was still looking around, when she heard a gasp from above. Jake stood at the top of the stairs.

"You're here," he said.

"I should have called," she said.

He came down the stairs. Lauren watched each step he took, wondering what she would say when he stood in front of her. She'd rehearsed a thousand different scenarios on her way to the apartment, but none of them came to mind as he approached.

"I didn't mean it," he said. "I didn't want you to leave."

"You didn't?"

"I'm in love with you."

"Wh… What?" she stammered.

"I've been in love with you since you showed up in the first of those silly outfits." He took her hand.

Lauren had been concentrating on his words, but his hand grabbed her attention.

"You moved it," she said, staring at his right hand holding hers.

"Because of you."

"Me?"

"It happened the day of the accident. I was so concerned about you that I didn't think. I opened the car door and you were slumped there behind the air bag. I had my cell phone in my hand before I knew I'd moved it."

Tears misted in her eyes, but she blinked them away. She smiled.

"This is wonderful," she said, running her hand over his arm.

"It's better than that." He pulled her to the sofa and they sat down. "I realized when you were around I wanted to be the man you saw me as being. Even if I never moved my hand again, I wanted your approval. I wanted you there every day."

"But you told me—"

"I know," he interrupted. "I just reacted, hadn't thought it all through. What it meant. What you're being here meant to me. Then I learned you were a doctor, and I was angry that you had lied to me."

She reached for his hand.

"I need you, Lauren. I know that it isn't

the good times that forge a couple. It's the bad times."

"We've have been through some of those," she said with a smile.

"You withstood it all. And when it came to me, you gave as good as you got. When I refused to do something, you cajoled me into doing it one way or another." He hung his head for a moment before looking at her. "I know I was wrong. When I found your room empty, I ran after you and the accident happened. Can you ever forgive me?"

"Forgive you? I'm the one who deceived you."

"I know and I understand you did it for a good reason. I should apologize for the way I treated you."

They gazed into each other's eyes for a long while and the tension between them broke. Laughter broke out. Grinning, Jake put his left arm around her shoulders. Lauren threaded her fingers through those on his right hand.

"I don't think I'll ever let this hand go," she said.

He gathered her closer. "I don't think I ever want you to. I love you."

"You know I'm in love with you too," Lauren said.

She felt him smile against her hair. "I thought as much, but it's so much better to actually hear the words." He leaned back and beamed at her. "Speaking of words, I have four more for you."

"The answer is yes," Lauren said, smiling, too.

* * * * *

For more romances from
Shirley Hailstock
and Harlequin Heartwarming,
visit www.Harlequin.com today!

Get 4 FREE REWARDS!

We'll send you 2 FREE Books plus 2 FREE Mystery Gifts.

Love Inspired® books feature contemporary inspirational romances with Christian characters facing the challenges of life and love.

FREE Value Over **$20**

Get 4 FREE REWARDS!

We'll send you 2 FREE Books plus 2 FREE Mystery Gifts.

Love Inspired® Suspense books feature Christian characters facing challenges to their faith... and lives.

FREE Value Over **$20**

YES! Please send me 2 FREE Love Inspired® Suspense novels and my 2 FREE mystery gifts (gifts are worth about $10 retail). After receiving them, if I don't wish to receive any more books, I can return the shipping statement marked "cancel." If I don't cancel, I will receive 6 brand-new novels every month and be billed just $5.24 each for the regular-print edition or $5.99 each for the larger-print edition in the U.S., or $5.74 each for the regular-print edition or $6.24 each for the larger-print edition in Canada. That's a savings of at least 13% off the cover price. It's quite a bargain! Shipping and handling is just 50¢ per book in the U.S. and $1.25 per book in Canada.* I understand that accepting the 2 free books and gifts places me under no obligation to buy anything. I can always return a shipment and cancel at any time. The free books and gifts are mine to keep no matter what I decide.

Choose one: ☐ **Love Inspired® Suspense**
Regular-Print
(153/353 IDN GNWN)

☐ **Love Inspired® Suspense**
Larger-Print
(107/307 IDN GNWN)

Name (please print)

Address   Apt. #

City   State/Province   Zip/Postal Code

Mail to the Reader Service:
IN U.S.A.: P.O. Box 1341, Buffalo, NY 14240-8531
IN CANADA: P.O. Box 603, Fort Erie, Ontario L2A 5X3

Want to try 2 free books from another series? Call 1-800-873-8635 or visit www.ReaderService.com.

THE FORTUNES OF TEXAS COLLECTION!

18 FREE BOOKS in all!

Treat yourself to the rich legacy of the Fortune and Mendoza clans in this remarkable 50-book collection. This collection is packed with cowboys, tycoons and Texas-sized romances!

YES! Please send me **The Fortunes of Texas Collection** in Larger Print. This collection begins with 3 FREE books and 2 FREE gifts in the first shipment. Along with my 3 free books, I'll also get the next 4 books from The Fortunes of Texas Collection, in LARGER PRINT, which I may either return and owe nothing, or keep for the low price of $5.24 U.S./$5.89 CDN each plus $2.99 for shipping and handling per shipment*. If I decide to continue, about once a month for 8 months I will get 6 or 7 more books but will only need to pay for 4. That means 2 or 3 books in every shipment will be FREE! If I decide to keep the entire collection, I'll have paid for only 32 books because 18 books are FREE! I understand that accepting the 3 free books and gifts places me under no obligation to buy anything. I can always return a shipment and cancel at any time. My free books and gifts are mine to keep no matter what I decide.

☐ 269 HCN 4622 ☐ 469 HCN 4622

Name (please print)

Address Apt. #

City State/Province Zip/Postal Code

Mail to the **Reader Service:**
IN U.S.A.: P.O. Box 1341, Buffalo, N.Y. 14240-8531
IN CANADA: P.O. Box 603, Fort Erie, Ontario L2A 5X3

50BFT19R

ReaderService.com has a new look!

We have refreshed our website and we want to share our new look with you. Head over to ReaderService.com and check it out!

On ReaderService.com, you can:

- Try 2 free books from any series
- Access risk-free special offers
- View your account history & manage payments
- Browse the latest Bonus Bucks catalog

Don't miss out!

If you want to stay up-to-date on the latest at the Reader Service and enjoy more Harlequin content, make sure you've signed up for our monthly News & Notes email newsletter. Sign up online at ReaderService.com.

INTRODUCING OUR
FABULOUS NEW COVER LOOK!
COMING FEBRUARY 2020

Find your favorite series in-store, online or subscribe to the Reader Service!